FANTASY

—

EDITED BY SEAN WALLACE

Bandersnatch, with Paul Tremblay
Best New Fantasy
Best New Fantasy 2
Horror: The Best of the Year, 2006 Edition
Horror: The Best of the Year, 2007 Edition
Jabberwocky 1
Jabberwocky 2
Jabberwocky 3
Japanese Dreams
Weird Tales

FANTASY

Edited by Sean Wallace & Paul Tremblay

PRIME BOOKS

FANTASY

Prime Books
www.prime-books.com
www.fantasy-magazine.com

For more information, contact **Prime Books.**

ISBN: 978-0-8095-5699-1

TABLE OF CONTENTS

———

INTRODUCTION

Within the pages of this anthology are eleven original works of short fiction of the type that can be found in every unique issue of *Fantasy Magazine*. A quarterly publication published by Prime Books and edited by the co-editors of this same anthology, *Fantasy Magazine* has, in the last two years, regaled readers with stories by Peter S. Beagle, Jeffrey Ford, Theodora Goss, Caitlin Kiernan, Stewart O'Nan, Tim Pratt, Margaret Ronald, Catherynne Valente, Jeff VanderMeer, and many more . . . mind you, all of them with sophisticated and literate tales that challenge the boundaries of imagination, and providing readers—those particularly with a love for language, for style, and for possibilities—with something original and fresh and exciting.

We sincerely hope that this anthology serves both as an introduction and as a sample of the kind of stories that we've published—and will publish—and hope that you find out for yourself why *Strange Horizons* calls *Fantasy Magazine* "quite wonderful and very exciting"—or why *Locus* calls it "one of the most promising new fiction publications to launch in the field in years."

—Sean Wallace & Paul Tremblay
www.fantasy-magazine.com

Margaret Ronald's fiction has appeared in Strange Horizons, Realms of Fantasy, Fantasy Magazine, *and* Ideomancer. *Originally from rural Indiana, she now lives outside Boston. She is an alumna of the Viable Paradise workshop and a member of BRAWL.*

"Goosegirl" originated with the fairy tale of the same name. I started thinking about some of the stranger elements in the story—the handkerchief spotted with blood, the stove as confessor—and about how one could choose to be part of a different story.

GOOSEGIRL

Margaret Ronald

I stumble into the city at the back of the princess's entourage, clutching the Red Book to my chest. By the time someone notices me, I can almost speak again.

"You came with the Princess Alia, didn't you?" says a tall man with an understeward's chain. "They must have low standards up north if you're the sort of thing she brings along."

I shake my head; the world slides in and out of focus. "I didn't come here for that. I'm not—help."

He raises his eyebrows. "Oh, so you're not with the help? You must be one of the nobility, then?" He tweaks my skirts, and a ragged hem tears. "So what did you come here for, if you're not with the princess?"

The words sound wrong even as I think them, but I say them nonetheless. "To be married."

He bursts out laughing. "Poor girl," a woman at the back of the servants' hall says. "She's simple. Can't tell between herself and the princess."

"No," I say, or try to say, but the words have come apart again, and it comes out in a rush of court poetry and gutter talk, unintelligible to noble and peasant alike.

The tall man laughs again and reaches for the Red Book. I skitter away, and a stink of pigs fills my nose. "Leave her be, Conrad," a man says behind me. His voice is deep and should not be familiar.

Conrad makes a face—whether from being thwarted or the smell I cannot tell. "I'll put her with the geese," he says, turning away. "They're about as dumb as she is. Just like you and your pigs."

"Just so," the swineherd says, and leans down to help me up. "Are you all right?"

"Yes, your majesty," I say, and cover my mouth.

He blinks, then laughs a second too late and helps me to my feet. I stare after him. I have never seen this man before, never seen his curls streaked with gray nor the somber, dark eyes. But I remember him—remember a portrait, presented to me, of the family of my betrothed.

But I have no betrothed. I am a hag, a witchwoman, and now a goosegirl.

At supper that night, I hear how the king could not attend the ceremonies greeting his new daughter-in-law. "He is ill much of the time now," says one of the understewards—not Conrad, Conrad is elsewhere. "So much so that the council meetings go on without him, with the prince in his place."

"Good that the prince is marrying, then," says another. "She's older than he; she'll teach him constancy."

"That'd take a miracle," another says, and laughs, though it is not nice laughter.

I peer down the table for the swineherd, but do not see him. I look at my plate, and my head swims; somewhere the food is swan's wing and plums, but here it is bread and dripping, and when I reach for it I miss, knocking it onto my dress.

Someone sighs, and I cover my face. "I came here to be married," I say to my palms, and cannot stop shaking.

There is work to do, and it cannot stop for one confused woman. Its rhythm aids me as the thumping beat of music aids a faltering dancer.

I ignore the marriage preparations, ignore the handsome prince and the beautiful princess and Conrad, and take the geese down to the river each day. There, I read the Red Book, learning it as I did before, once, maybe. It is not in a script I know—and that I could read other scripts surprises me, for am I not a goosegirl only? But nonetheless I can read it, and this tells me one other thing: only a witch could read these blotted brown words. So I know what I must be.

The Red Book's words are mutable—one, *to deter*, can mean:

> to prevent sickness entering into a wound;
> to keep midges from clustering around one's face;
> or to distract Conrad so he will stop tweaking my skirts.

Or there is *to poison*, which can mean:

to wilt the weeds in a field while leaving the barley
    untouched;
to sour a cask of beer with a glance;
or to turn a person's heart against a loved one.

I study the words, day by day at the river, and ignore the meaningless courtiers' chatter of geese. The Red Book is powerful; I remember my crabbed and wizened mother the witch warning me of it on her deathbed. She pressed the stained linen pages into my hands and cautioned me to use it well, for I had a wild look, and she feared what I might do.

But this I also remember: my stately and sorrowful mother the queen pricking her finger and letting three drops fall upon a swan-white handkerchief. She pressed the blotted linen into my hands and cautioned me never to lose it, for I had a long journey to make, and she feared for my safety. And I cannot remember which mother is mine, nor which I love.

I press the heels of my hands to my eyes. Did I leave my mother's home in a great procession, off to the castle of my betrothed, there to make a new life? Or did I leave my mother's home in dead of night, following the lights of a far caravan, determined to use the Book to write myself a new life?

The procession itself is a snarl of images, inextricable. I remember a new maidservant, a foreign princess, a fallen handkerchief and a chalice spilling water, remember words spoken and heard. But which words?

There is another word in the Red Book: *to cleave*, which

means to make one where there were two, or two where there was one. I do not understand this word.

For some time I cannot believe that no one else has guessed the swineherd's secret: how he works only when the king is sick, how he contrives to be away should the prince come calling among the maidservants, how the lines of his profile are reflected on the coin of the realm. But when they speak of the king, they always call him old, and this is his greatest disguise: not a smock and artfully applied dirt, but his relative youth. He is no more than twelve years older than I; he fathered the prince young and was widowed young. (And I, no matter which memory I touch, know I was old to be married: past twenty at least.) Maybe they confuse the king with his father, who died only a year ago and whose endless senescence has endowed the crown with years; maybe the vitality of the prince steals any youth from his surroundings. Or maybe it is only that no one cares to look too closely at one who reeks of pigs.

He finds me practicing my witchery down by the river, shaping a stone and causing grass figures to dance, and though it is enough to have me cast out of the palace, he does not denounce me. Instead he is fascinated, and tells me of times he met witches on his wanderings, and laughs for sheer joy when I spin last year's leaves into a whirlwind.

No one has ever admired me for what I can do. Only for what I was. I think of the heavy weight of brocade and shake my sleeves back to give my hands more freedom.

On the days that I take the geese down to the river, he joins me, and we sit together on the mud-slick banks. When the world shivers around me, he tells me stories till the fit passes, stories of going forth to seek his fortune, of ogres and conjurers and treasure hidden beneath wandering stones. I smile and do not tell him that a swineherd is unlikely to have had such adventures.

There is always a spot that he forgets to dirty, just past where his graying curls end. On the prince this spot is always covered by high collars and rich cloaks. His father the king tugs the neck of his shirt open and gazes at the sky and has not found the fortune he sought.

The north gate of the palace is the grandest, and it is through there that most of the traffic passes. Three days before the wedding, I drive my charges through it for the first time and hear a grinding moan, as though the wall itself were crying out.

A small shrine of the horse goddess Epona is cut into the gate to bless all who travel through, and it is this that has spoken. A horse's head, carved in weathered stone, struggles to speak around its bit and bridle. *Child, if your mother knew,* it groans, *her royal heart would break in two.*

I stop dead, the geese milling about me like baffled children. To either side, the traffic continues unabated; no one else has heard the horse's cry.

"Epona," I say, but it does not speak again. And it does not need to—I remember now, why it might speak to me, for I was named for the horse-goddess. But was it a queen or a witch who named me so?

My heart is not so delicate as a queen's, I think, because I am not royal. Or perhaps it is that I am already broken.

The king in a swineherd's smock has escaped his court for the day, and thus I have company on the riverbank. I know enough not to call him majesty now, and he is good enough not to recall my one error. He carries water in his hat as we coax our charges back to the castle, and I laugh at him. He laughs too, and for a moment there is no chasm in my mind, or none that matters.

We reach the gate, but the prince and princess are there before us, returning from the hunt. The prince on his charger hurtles past, heedless and beautiful; briefly I catch a wistful look on the king's face. The princess rides behind, regal as the queen she will one day be. She looks at me, then at the king. She is not easily fooled.

Unnerved, I edge closer to the gate, too close to Epona's shrine. The stone horse moans its lament, and I cringe. The king does not quite hear, but it seems some of his tales are true, for he cocks his head as if straining after a whisper.

The princess shakes her reins, glances back at me, and rides through. I stare after her and cannot speak; the words tangle again, and worse now.

In the middle of the night I wake and hear another persons breathing. I speak a word: *to see*, and light pools in my hand. The unseen person gasps, and I sit up, brushing straw from my hair.

The princess sits on a stool by the door. She holds the hem of her dress an inch above the floor, and her eyes follow the light in my hands. "I know what you are trying to do," she says. "It won't work."

"What am I trying to do?" I ask.

"I've ordered that the shrine be removed. You won't have it as witness any more." I say nothing, and her voice rises, warbling high and scared. "I am a princess now. I can have you executed. I will have you executed, if you tell a living soul."

A sweet, damp breeze drifts in with a grumble of thunder, and I think of the riverbank, which will be impassable mud tomorrow. "What could I tell them?" I say. "I do not know what I was—witch, halfwit, princess?" The last makes her blanch. "Princess," I repeat, tasting the word that used to be familiar. Was I ever so frightened as she is now?

"Princess no longer. Now you are a common goose-girl."

In the whites of her eyes, too bright in this light, I see that I am not the only one with split memories. The spell she worked to switch us has shattered her as well, though she at least can talk. But she is only a princess now.

I remember being a princess, when being was required more than acting. The Red Book is under my pillow; I want to touch its pages, reassure myself that it is still there. I gesture with the light in my hand. "Why? Why change one for the other?"

I mean the knowledge, the witchery, the Red Book and all that goes with it. But she looks to the light's glare on the walls, the trickle of water under the shutters, the dirty straw of my pallet. "Why?" she laughs. "Look at it! I'd give it all up again—I'd lie beneath a thousand men to escape this!"

I pause, thinking to tell her of the gossip in the servants' hall. Conrad at least is honest; if a maid beds him, he will find

16

her a station in the castle. The prince is known for sending his bedmates away, or worse. (Such things were not mentioned in the betrothal agreement, but they are discussed freely here.) But she is a princess, and she will wed him; perhaps it will be different.

She mistakes my hesitation. "You can't have him," she says. "He doesn't want you."

"I don't want him." What I want is a clear head and uncluttered memories. But there is only one road to that, only one ending to the story we have woven: the impostor's cruel death, the princess' return, the wedding. How high is the price for a mind made whole?

The princess rises, gathering her skirts. "I will have you killed," she says. "Remember that, princess."

I start at the word. She turns scarlet, covers her mouth, and flees. Her footsteps fade into the patter of rain outside, and I am left with my light and my split mind.

The rain is heavy and cold, and even though I run the short distance to the swineherd's hut, my dress is sodden and clinging to me by the time I reach it. I close the door behind me, and my eyes slowly take in the emptiness of the hut. He is not here—of course, he is in the castle, trying to be a king.

And even if he were here, I decide, I would not tell him. This is my story, not his, and any other reason I came here is now not worth considering. I cannot remember if I have lain with a man—the princess certainly not, the witch certainly—but what I seek tonight is more than the comfort of skin on skin. Still, the rain comes down hard, and I pluck at my dress, unwilling to go back out.

Though the swineherd must perforce stay away from this hut most nights, the hearth is swept clean, and before it he has set up a little shrine of lares, household gods. Epona is there, and Moccus of swineherds and kings both, and the Lugoves. I sit before them, dripping onto the hard earth, and I tell them all. Though Epona could not help me (if returning my name to me was not help), I can still ask, still confide in the old gods.

My hair is drying when I have finished my tale, though my face is wet. But the hearth remains cold, and my prayers are flat, and the rain does not abate.

I have erred. I do not realize how badly I have erred until a footman shows me to a room too opulent for my tattered skirts. He leaves, and a figure rises from the chair by the window. "Princess," he calls me.

Perhaps in my confusion I did not see him in the shadows of the hut; perhaps it was empty, and he came later to listen at the chimney; perhaps, even, Moccus the patron of kings and swineherds decided to send my prayers to the man who follows both his paths. This last, I think, is most likely; the lares, when they answer prayers, do so smiling.

The crown's gleam does little to offset the lines it forces in his brow; the velvet robes drain his hair of color and reduce iron-gray to silver-gray. He greets me, royalty to royalty, and laments my state, and promises to return me to my former position. And yet his face says other things, things a swineherd would say without hesitation but a king may not.

I nod but do not answer him. I have not spoken since arriving; instead I watch the fall of light over his shoulders and think of things broken. The Red Book, tucked into my bodice, presses heavy over my heart, and my skin smells of mud and last night's rain.

"I cannot let my son marry an impostor," he says.

How high is the price for a mind made whole?

I cannot pay with another's life. I have only myself for coin.

"If you were to do this," I say at last, "if you were to expose her crime and elevate me to her place, then I would be the impostor."

He tilts his head to the side, the same way he did when the stone horses spoke.

"I am no princess. I was, and am not." My feet grow heavier, as if sinking through the floor, and one by one the memories of my mother the queen fade, till they are like pictures traced in dust. And surely it is dust that makes my eyes water now, to mourn the loss of a woman I never knew. Still I speak, swallowing back salt tears. "I am a witchwoman, and I will not give that up for any cause."

The Red Book burns against my chest and is gone. I cry out and put my hand to where it was, then feel it again—its words my blood now, its pages my flesh. It writes itself in me, as the story is unwritten and unraveling.

The king steps forward to catch me, afraid perhaps that a princess might faint. I let him take me by the shoulders. "You too have a choice," I say, and look up at him. "If you trust me, you have a choice."

The prince's wedding day is a week past, but already the servants are replacing the banners with swathes of black cloth.

The king, too weak to leave his bed, blesses the prince and princess and charges them with the care of the kingdom.

I stand outside the gates, the air thick with my magic, and speak one word: *to cleave*. The king's eyes close at last, and the prince rises from his bedside, impatient to begin ruling. The princess lingers a moment, staring down at the body as if she might see some trace of magic on it. But she is a princess, now a queen, who has what she always wanted and cannot read the marks of witchery.

Beside me, the swineherd shudders and lets out a long breath. He rises, feeling how his body moves, how it differs from what was. I speak the second word: *to cleave*, and I take his hand. We walk out of the city, our fortune before us.

Becca De La Rosa is studying English at university in Dublin. Her work has appeared, among other places, at Strange Horizons *and* LCRW.

ALL THE GROWING TIME

Becca De La Rosa

Isolde Martial and My Lord Yesterday have two important similarities, although they are, by nature, entirely different. Firstly: Isolde Martial and My Lord Yesterday both have pet black birds named Jacqueline. These birds are not sisters, although there is some ongoing debate as to whether they might in fact be the same bird. And secondly: both My Lord Yesterday and Isolde Martial collect time.

Isolde Martial and My Lord Yesterday met for the first time in Venice, although they were not really meeting for the first time, because they had known each other forever. He was in a gondola. She was dressed up like a doctor, with a bird beak nose made of papier maché. She burned herbs in her long black nose. To My Lord Yesterday she smelled of salt and rosemary smoke.

There are three books written on the subject of their first conversation; these books are called *The Kiss of Certain Spiders*, *Light Fantastic*, and *The History and Development of Organised Crime in Midwestern Suburbia: An Anthropological Study*. I have read these books, but do not recommend them. No one remembers what Isolde Martial and My Lord Yesterday said to each other. I used to know, but I have forgotten. It was such a long time ago.

My Lord Yesterday and Isolde Martial spent two weeks underneath the Bridge of Sighs, in a boat made of cork wood and streaming with satin ribbons, and if you need to ask me how they passed the time, you have no kind of imagination at all.

Isolde Martial is tall and thin. Her hair looks like a telephone cable. Isolde Martial lost an eye in Finland; she left in on her bedside table at night, and when she woke up in the morning it was gone. Isolde Martial believes a magpie took it. This is only one of the reasons for her ongoing feud with the magpies. I do not know the other. Isolde Martial made a new eye out of an egg-shaped garnet, which she kept on a chain around her neck while she slept, and which stained her cheeks red when she stood in sunlight. Isolde Martial will sing for you all fifty-six verses of Child's ninth 'Tam Lin', if you ask her. Don't ask her.

My Lord Yesterday wears his bones outside his body. They rattle like maracas when he walks. This is how you can hear him coming. His bones used to be stiff as glass, but they drank water from the air, and soaked up sun, and began to twine around him, to put out leaves. His bones look like vines now. It is his skin that looks like bone: it is hard, ossified, and breaks when he falls or when you hit him. Through the fractures in his skin you can see rich brown soil. My Lord Yesterday drinks maple syrup out of pewter goblets. He bakes poetry in his oven to eat for his supper. My Lord Yesterday does not smile very often, but when he does, it is like sunrise in Venice.

———

After two weeks together Isolde Martial and My Lord Yesterday fought badly. She sank his boat, and he swallowed her garnet eye. Jacqueline pecked at Jacqueline until black feathers littered the canal. My Lord Yesterday swore he would never see Isolde Martial again, and swam away, with Jacqueline sitting on his head like a queen.

Isolde Martial never cries, not even when her father died in the fire, not even when she lost her eye. She does not have the time to cry. Isolde Martial and Jacqueline found a boat to sail them to France. They sat on deck together, watching sunset after sunset steal the horizon.

Neither Isolde Martial nor My Lord Yesterday is greedy. They do not collect time just so they can have and horde it, so they can run it through their fingers and count its grains. If they did, this would be a very different kind of story, and I would not be the one to tell it. So listen.

My Lord Yesterday gathers seconds in the pouch hanging from his right hip bone. He carries them to his home on the horizon and plants them in the earth. He feeds them water and sunlight and a fine meal made of ground grey bones, and they grow up sweet and strong, into minutes, hours, days. He guards them carefully. Their branches are always neatly trimmed. When they are ripe, they fall off the vine and into the earth, and they become the days and weeks and years you live in. The sun rises and sets in My Lord Yesterday's garden. Cultivating time is not an easy job, but My Lord Yesterday loves a challenge.

Isolde Martial eats lost time. Her teeth are small and strong. She is walking behind you, counting the heartbeats until you make a mistake, until you do something you will regret later on. Isolde Martial is always hungry. She eats lost time like cotton candy. It melts away to nothing in her mouth.

The first dead man washed up in My Lord Yesterday's horizon home five days after Isolde Martial sailed away. This was strange for many reasons, but most of all because My Lord Yesterday's home is nowhere near the water. The dead man wore a long blue coat, black boots, a belt made of silk threads and pieces of silver. There was a round sapphire in his mouth. When he tried to speak, the sapphire bobbed up and down. The dead man spat it out. "I am terribly sorry," he said, "but might I trouble you for a glass of water? My throat is very dry."

My Lord Yesterday walked stiffly up to his house. By the time he came back, carrying a watering can, the dead man had stopped moving. His eyes were shut.

My Lord Yesterday washed the dead man's face and hands. He burned the corpse on a bonfire of time, dry branches that crackled like fireworks and stained the horizon with scents of smoke, earth, and burning herbs.

Everything burned to ash except the dead man's heart and his round sapphire. My Lord Yesterday planted the heart in a flower patch, and it grew up into a cherry tree; its branches were long and elegant, but the fruit always tasted of soot and blood. My Lord Yesterday strung the sapphire on a chain around his neck.

He sat and thought, and he thought: *dead men do not wash*

up here every day, which they didn't, and *Isolde Martial is gone*, which she was. He sat and he sat. The sun hovered at twelve o'clock, watching him. The world hovered at twelve o'clock. My Lord Yesterday stopped thinking.

The second dead man appeared in Isolde Martial's cabin aboard the *Chestnut Lady* when they were only a half-day's sail from Marseille. The dead man sat on her bunk and smoked a black cigar. He was dead. His skin was mottled and blue like a tray of mismatched puzzle pieces, all sky. He said, "Had I but known, Tam Lin, Tam Lin," and then watched Isolde Martial expectantly.

Isolde Martial was very polite. She asked him what he was doing in her bed. The dead man did not answer. He was dead, after all. There was a ruby in his mouth where his words should have been.

Isolde Martial and Jacqueline pulled the dead man out on deck and dropped him in the ocean. He floated like a lobster trap. Isolde Martial watched him for the next six hours, feasting on the time the other passengers shed behind them in glossy snail-tracks; she watched fish taste his fingers, and tangle in his hair, and finally steal his eyes. Isolde Martial cried then. She knew what that was like. Her tears fell into the time she was eating and made the mixture sweeter.

And one, two, three weeks passed. Isolde Martial bought a house in Marseilles, and out her bedroom window she could see strands of lost time glisten on the trees and pavement like golden syrup, tantalising and fresh, but Isolde Martial had lost her appetite. Jacqueline worried. She flew out at dawn and returned with her claws full of tasty morsels, but Isolde Martial just drifted from room to room to room. Lost time pooled up in the cracks of the world. Children began to fall down into it. If you were a child and you fell into a rockpool of lost time, you could stay forever that way, a fly in amber, waiting to be born. I once met two children who had drowned in lost time. "What was it like?" I asked. "We knew all the secrets in the world," the girl said. The boy said, "When they pulled us out we forgot everything."

My Lord Yesterday wove wicker baskets out of time and sailed away in them. He was gone long, long, longer. Jacqueline flew out every day to see him, although the basket tossed and dipped and made her seasick. Jacqueline brought him flasks of sweet green tea and packets of nuts and dried apples. Mostly he just watched the sea; his face became like the sea. Dead men waved to him from underneath the water.

Time grew bolder, and began to play tricks on the world. Once it stayed Monday for seventeen days in a row. Midnight began to come right after dawn, which came right after four in the afternoon. Clocks and watches broke from too much winding. Only the dead were untroubled. The dead have very little use for time.

Mister Death climbed over the mountains on his four long legs. He shed his skin at My Lord Yesterday's house on the horizon. Swearing loudly, Mister Death stepped over the water to where My Lord Yesterday sat in his wicker basket. "Boy, you're being very difficult," he said.

My Lord Yesterday blinked at him. He said nothing.

"All your spare time is cracking roots down into the heart

of the world. The dead are finding their way up through the tunnels it has made," Mister Death said. "All this time, all this overgrown time. The dead are taking the heart of the world with them. In their pockets. In their mouths. How selfish are the young and the dead. It is a fine time for jewellers, my boy, but hard days for Mister Death."

My Lord Yesterday touched the sapphire strung around his neck. It drummed like blood. He glanced away, back at the sea.

"Oh, my boy," said Mister Death. "Well. On we must go." He lifted My Lord Yesterday in his thin hands, cradled him close to his chest, where My Lord Yesterday could hear all the heartbeats of the world. Mister Death carried him across the ocean.

If you asked politely, I would tell you about Mister Death. I would start by telling you about his eyes. I would not compare them to pomanders or mussel shells or black glass from the bottom of the bottle. I would describe for you his fingers, how they are not like cobwebs stiff with frozen dew, not like pokers heated on the fire, especially not like any kind of broom or bramble. You would know about his long, long, long smile. Which is in no way like the coffin they bury you in. Despite what you might be told.

Isolde Martial and Jacqueline grew tired of Marseilles. They gathered their things into a burlap sack and set sail for Ireland, which is the place you go when you have run out of ideas. The journey was long and grey. A dead man sat down beside them up on the deck one night. Isolde Martial did not scream or speak, and the woman and the dead man watched each other for a long time, as though both were waiting for something to happen, although neither of them knew what. His mouth was closed around a black tourmaline.

All day and all night the dead drifted over the ship. They clacked their finger bones in a song or a secret code. The other passengers did not know what to say, so they said very little. Once Isolde Martial woke to find a dead man in her bed, whispering something around the jewel in his mouth, the heart in his mouth. He grinned at her. Isolde Martial pushed him to the other side of the bed and went back to sleep. She has had to deal with stranger things, although I don't know what they are.

Mister Death fed My Lord Yesterday tree-sap and milky roots. He sang to him in his dead voice. Then he took My Lord Yesterday to the top of the world, and showed him the thick jungles of time that stretched out on the horizon. "This is all your fault, my boy," said Mister Death, and gave him a shovel, and marched away.

My Lord Yesterday set to work.

At first time was angry. It coiled around My Lord Yesterday's feet, to trip and trap him. It wanted freedom. But My Lord Yesterday worked and worked, and he dug gullies and poured sweet rosé wine down to the roots of time, and he trimmed away dead leaves and branches. The time remembered how it loved My Lord Yesterday. It purred and settled. Thick vines of it parted to let him pass. My Lord Yesterday sang to time, very gently. The dead heard his song (the dead love music). They followed it, across the horizon, down into the heart of the world, and Mister Death wrapped his long arms around them, and called them his children.

And Isolde Martial looked into Ireland and saw her own reflection. It made her uncomfortable, how Ireland was like a mirror or a flat ocean, and so she lay down on the ground, rippling the country with her dreams. Jacqueline made friends with the dead. They fed her handfuls of barley and jewel chips. Jacqueline would eat anything.

When My Lord Yesterday had finished working, and when the world had settled back into its rhythms, he bobbed out to sea in his wicker basket again. The winds were strong at his back. Jacqueline flew ahead of him. He followed a path of black feathers on the water.

Isolde Martial saw him coming. She saw him coming, stained with dirt, looped with seaweed like a skipping rope, his hair full of sprigs of time, his pockets full of sand. When he kissed her she tasted time on his lips.

My Lord Yesterday took the sapphire from around his neck and offered it to Isolde Martial. She fitted the jewel in her eye, and now she can see out of it, and she sees the secrets of the dead, and the heart of everything.

And now when Isolde Martial stands behind you, waiting to catch your lost time, she ticks like a clock. She taps like hot oil in a pan. She is the heartbeat of the world. Isolde Martial is not an eloquent woman, but if you ask, she will tell you this story. She will start at the beginning. Once upon a time, she will say, while she is spinning your lost time onto a spool, while the world drums at her eye, beat-beat-beat.

Sarah Monette grew up in Oak Ridge, Tennessee, one of the three secret cities of the Manhattan Project. Having completed her Ph.D. in English literature, she now lives and writes in a 101-year-old house in the Upper Midwest. Her novels are published by Ace Books. Her short fiction has appeared in many places, including Strange Horizons, Alchemy, *and* Lady Churchill's Rosebud Wristlet.

"Somewhere Beneath Those Waves Was Her Home" was inspired partly by a necklace made by the breathtakingly talented Elise Matthesen—the title, in fact, comes from the necklace—and partly by a figurehead in the collection of the Art Institute of Chicago. The selkie walked in on her own two (unwanted) feet.

SOMEWHERE BENEATH THOSE WAVES WAS HER HOME

Sarah Monette

184. Figurehead. Wood. 35" x 18". American, ca. 1850. Figure of a woman holding a telescope and compass. Ship unknown.

The selkie stands at the window, staring out at the sea. Behind her, in the rumpled bed, the artist snores. She's had better sex with her own fingers, but it doesn't matter. He wanted it, and it amuses her to cheat on Byron. In their stalemate—she cannot make him give back her skin, he cannot make her love him—she takes her pleasures where she finds them.

She sighs, running one palm over her velvet-short hair. It would've been nice if the artist fucked as pretty as he talks.

197. Figurehead. Wood. 34" x 17". American, ca. 1830-35. Figure of a woman in a hat. Ship unknown.

I found a museum today. Not a surprise, really, but I'd given up on there being anything interesting to do in this town. The only bookstore for twenty miles was a rare and used dealer along the "picturesque" main street specializing in the most abstruse and technical aspects of naval history. I'd spent hours on the beach, staring at the water and the gulls. The water was dark; the gulls were blindingly white. And malicious, I thought. They would have appreciated me more if I'd been dead, and I saw that truth in their little, bright eyes.

But this afternoon I turned up a side street, and there was the sign: **MARITIME MUSEUM.** I'd taken it for a warehouse. It was open, and I needed something to do for at least one of the three hours remaining before I could legitimately go back to the apartment Dale had rented and begin to wait for him. I pushed open the door, and pushed hard, for like all the doors in this town it was balky and swollen with the breath of the sea.

I'd been in more than my share of maritime museums, as Dale had a passion for them. This one seemed indistinguishable from the multitude: bleak and dusty and full of ship models and scrimshaw and all the sad mortal paraphernalia of a long-gone way of life. I stood for a long time before a case of glass pyramids, once set in the decks of ships to allow light into the cramped spaces below. I wondered how long you would have to stay down there before you forgot that you could not reach up your hand and touch the sun.

The museum's collection was large, but not terribly interesting. "Thorough" would be the polite word. There was nothing there I hadn't seen better examples of elsewhere, and I was unhappily conscious that the museum was not occupying enough of the long brazen afternoon. I walked more and more slowly, carefully reading each word of each printed placard, and still I was calculating: how long to finish at the museum, how long to walk back to the apartment, how long to take a shower. How long I'd waited for Dale the previous night and all the nights before.

And then I turned a corner, stepped through a narrow doorway, and found myself in a long hall, its stretch of narrow windows admitting dusty sunlight and a view of the sea; a hall bare except for the double row of figureheads, mounted like the caryatids of some great invisible temple.

I started down the hall, reading the placard beside each figurehead and studying awkward proportions, stiff shoulders, clumsily carved faces. The collection was composed entire of women: naked, half-dressed, clothed in Sunday best; blonde and brunette and redheaded; empty-handed and holding books and holding navigational instruments. And all of them staring, their eyes seeming to seek for something lost and irreplaceable, something that they would never find in this half-neglected room.

There was a feeling of incompleteness about them. They had never been meant to be seen on their own, nor from this unnatural angle. Their makers had intended them to be part of a greater whole, had intended them to lean forward fiercely, joyfully, into the crash and billow of the sea. By rights they were the eyes, the spirits, of ships far vaster than themselves. This room was not where they belonged; this room was not their home.

The dust motes floating in the shafts of sunlight, the long shallow gouges in the floor boards, the cracking, yellowing plaster of the walls—I had never been in a room so sad. The figureheads seemed like mourners, standing at the edges of a grave which was the aisle I walked down. For a moment, I felt truly buried alive, in my marriage, in this town, in this dreary, dusty hall.

But even as my heart pounded against my ribs, my breath coming short from imagined suffocation, I looked into the face of a figurehead whose long wooden hair was entwined with strands of wooden pearls, and saw that I was not the one buried in this room. Nor was I the one for whom they grieved, the one for whom they watched. They were waiting for something that could not enter the museum to find them.

After I worked my way up one side and down the other, I returned to stand in front of one woman, the pale green of sea-foam, her prim Victorian maiden's face framing the wide-open eyes of an ecstatic visionary. I was staring into her eyes, trying to put a name to what I saw there, when I was startled nearly out of my wits by a man's voice asking, "Do you like the figureheads, miss?"

After the silence of the figureheads, the man's harsh voice seemed as brutal as the roar of a noreaster. I turned around. The door at the far end of the hall, marked "EMPLOYEES ONLY," was open, and a tall, gaunt old man stood with his hand on the knob. His hair was iron-gray, clipped short, and he wore jeans and a cable-knit sweater.

"Yes," I said, groping after my composure. "They . . . they are very beautiful."

"Aye," he said, coming toward me, and I had to repress the stupid impulse to back away, "they are. There's nothing like them made any more." When he reached me, he extended his hand. "Ezekiel Pitt."

I shook hands with him, although I didn't want to. It was like shaking hands with a tangle of hawsers, even down to the faint sensation of grime left on my palm and fingers when he let go. I refrained with an effort from wiping my hand on my jeans. "Magda Fenton."

"Nice to meet you, Miss Fenton," Ezekiel Pitt said politely, and I did not correct him. "I do most of the collecting for the museum, and I must admit the ladies have always been my favorite." His smile was unpleasant, the teeth prominent and yellow and wolf-like. His smell was musty and sweaty at once, and I gave in and backed up a step.

"Why do none of them have names?" I had noticed that on the placards; figurehead after figurehead was *ship unknown*.

"They're all from shipwrecks, these ladies," Ezekiel Pitt said. "Their names are beneath the sea, like their ships. I suppose you might call them widows."

"Yes, you might," I said, although it seemed to me, looking at their wide, blind eyes, that it would be fairer to call them lost spirits, sundered from their proud bodies, their unbounded blue world, their joyous wooden lives.

Ezekiel Pitt was crowding me again, and I did not like him. I moved toward the door, to finish my tour of this dismal museum and return to my dismal life. He stayed where he was; out of the corner of my eye, I saw him touch the green woman's face, caressing it like a lover. At the door, I stopped. I had one question more. "Why are they all women?"

He glanced up from the green woman and gave me a horrible, unbelievable, leering wink. "I only like the ladies, miss," he said.

I could stand him and his sad prisoners no longer; I fled.

179. Figurehead. Wood. 32" x 17". American, ca. 1840. Figure of a woman crowned with flowers. Ship unknown.

Byron Pitt stole the selkie's skin on an August afternoon when the sky was dull with heat, the sun as fake as an arcade token and not a cloud near to cover its shame.

Byron knows the old stories either far too well or not nearly well enough. He ran with her skin that first day, ran like an ungainly jackrabbit, and nothing—nothing within the limited compass of what she is allowed—will make him tell her what he did with it. She cannot hurt him, much as she would like to; she cannot leave him. She *could* refuse to have sex with him, but it would do her no good. Byron is willfully stupid about a lot of things, but not even he is foolish enough to believe she would stay with him one split-second past the moment she got her hands on her skin again. And although selkies can lie, it is not natural to them: she admits the truth of her own appetites. Even Byron is better than no one at all.

But he isn't enough. He could never be enough, even if she loved him as the stories say some selkies came to love their captors. And she doesn't even like him, although much to her own irritation, she finds him too pathetic to hate. She's all he's ever had, he tells her over and over again, and it's all too easy to believe.

She doesn't care about charity. She wants her damn skin back. Her life. Her home.

In the six months she's been trapped on land, she's trashed Byron's apartment twice, searching. Her skin isn't there. She's explored this dreary town as thoroughly as she ever explored the sunken ships that were her childhood playground. She knows everywhere Byron goes, and she's searched all those places, too. All of them except for one.

She knows her skin is in the Maritime Museum, the same way she knows, not quite in her head and not quite in her gut, where her sisters are, out in the cold Atlantic. It may not be true, this knowing, but it's real. These days, it's the most real thing about her.

But she can't go into the museum. The museum is Ezekiel Pitt's territory, and her fear of him is too deep for reason.

Ezekiel is Byron's uncle or cousin or something like that. He knows what she is, knew the moment he laid eyes on her, without Byron saying a word, and he doesn't care. He's not impressed, not appalled; he looks at her as if she's just another curio in the museum, and not even an interesting one. But the way he looks at Byron . . . Ezekiel Pitt may not care about selkies, but he understands Byron perfectly. He knows what it is to keep something that doesn't belong to you. Knows and gloats, and she knows it was Ezekiel who put the idea of catching a selkie into Byron's stupid head.

She fears him because she does not understand him and because whenever she sees him, she smells death in captivity, smells the truth, that Byron is never going to let her go. Ezekiel

Pitt makes her want to submit, to let Byron take her self the way he took her skin, and that scares her most of all.

191. *Figurehead. Wood. 45" x 15". American, ca. 1840. Figure of a woman using a telescope. Ship unknown.*

That night, lying beside Dale's indifference, I dreamed of the figureheads. They were free from their mountings, standing at the windows of their prison, staring out at the clamoring surf. The moonlight showed the tears on their faces, showed their small pleading wooden hands pressed against the indifferent glass. And then, in my dream, like a gull I flew out from the museum, out over the dark and terrible sea. I flew for miles and miles without becoming tired or afraid, marveling in the beauty of the water and the night.

Then I dove beneath the waves. I seemed still to be flying, effortlessly, down through the water, and I knew I was a seal, as much at home in this element as gulls were in the air. I reached the sea floor and there danced in and out of the gaping, barnacle-encrusted hulls of sunken ships. These were the ships of the figureheads, their lives and their deaths, all here interred in the sand beneath the black weight of the water.

188. *Figurehead. Wood. 37" x 22". American, 1865? Figure of a woman holding a broken chain. Ship unknown.*

The selkie spends a lot of time on the beach. It drives Byron up the wall; he seems to be afraid that someone will figure out what she is and take her away from him. "Well, I can hope," the selkie said, and Byron winced and shut up.

She met the artist on the beach, let him think he was seducing her. She's learned a lot, these last few months, about the lies men tell themselves.

She pushes the cuffs of her sweat pants up and walks as far into the tide as she can in this stupid body that will drown if she lets it, or die of cold. She doesn't swim; without her skin, it's just a mockery.

She stands for a long time, until her feet start to go numb, and it's not until she turns back toward the land that she realizes she's not alone. There's a woman standing at the high tide line.

The selkie startles, splashing. The woman doesn't even seem to notice, and as the selkie wades back to dry land, she realizes that the woman is crying. The selkie skirts wide around her, light-headed with relief when she makes it to the public parking lot without attracting the woman's attention. She glances back, and the woman is still standing there. Staring out to sea, crying slow silent tears, as if the oceans of her body are trying to find their way home.

176. Figurehead. Wood. 39" x 19". American, ca. 1820. Figure of a Native American woman. Ship unknown.

I woke up hard, my breath caught in my throat, rolled over and looked at the clock. It was almost six a.m. I couldn't stand the stifling closeness of the bedroom any longer; I got up, dragged on yesterday's clothes, and escaped into the open. Dale always slept like the dead, and he wouldn't care even if he woke. I took the same path I'd taken for days, threading my way through the stiff, sullen town to the beach. I stood there, just above the undulation of seaweed that marked the high tide line, staring at the jeweled golden mystery of the sunrise, my mind, still half-dreaming, full of the memory of the figureheads, imprisoned in a hall as stifling as that bedroom, held away from the place where they belonged. The green woman's childlike face returned to me, her rapturous eyes.

Somewhere beneath those waves was her home. The rich strangeness, the terrible sadness of the dream returned to me, and I realized that I was crying, hot silent tears sliding down my cheeks; I licked one off my upper lip, but could not distinguish its taste from the salt miasma of the sea. I stared at the water until my eyes felt as sea-blasted and blind as the figureheads', and then I began to walk, aimlessly, blindly, my mind in the air with the gulls, in the deep water with the seals, in the dusty prison with the waiting women.

190. Figurehead. Wood. 30" x 18". American, ca. 1870-1890. Figure of a mermaid. Ship unknown.

The selkie answers the phone: "Moonwoman Coffeehouse."

"Hi, Russet, it's me. Byron." Byron always has to name both of them when he calls her, as if he has to guard against the possibility that their identities might slip. She feels sorry for him, for the crippled understanding that thinks identity has anything to do with something as arbitrary as a name. *Russet* isn't her name anyway, but it'll do.

"Hello, Byron," she says warily.

"Look," Byron said, his voice a little too high, a little too fast, "I've been thinking. I think we should get married."

She wants to laugh at him, but she can't find the breath. Because marriage means Byron isn't getting tired of this horrible fake relationship, isn't coming to his senses. No, quite the opposite: Byron wants to make it *official*.

She hears herself say, "Well, we can't talk about it now, Jesus, Byron!" And watches her hand, small and broad and brown, hang up the phone. And then she starts to shake.

She looks up, and Shelly is staring at her. "You okay?"

"Yeah. Just Byron, y'know?"

Shelly says, "I wish you'd just go ahead and dump his ass," and the selkie gives her half a smile and a shrug and gets back to work.

She clears tables and scrubs counters all morning, remembering to smile at the regulars, remembering receipts and correct change and to keep out of Shelly's way as she works. She has the afternoon off. She doesn't have another meeting with the artist until next week. Byron won't be home 'til six. She walks to the museum after eating a lunch she doesn't taste, and then stands in front of the door for nearly five minutes, trying to stop shaking. Ezekiel Pitt isn't interested in her. The worst he'll do is tell Byron, and she isn't afraid of Byron. Byron's power over her is only a matter of her skin and the old stupid rules about possessing it. Nothing here can hurt her, so why can't she move?

Because she's afraid. She's afraid of Ezekiel Pitt; she's afraid of the museum where he dens. Her fear is brutal, terrible, so vast she can't even run from it. She stands, wooden and helpless, on the sidewalk until a voice says, "Are you all right?" and breaks her stasis.

It's the woman from the beach, the pale, mousy woman

who was watching the sunrise and crying, and this time the selkie is close enough that even a stupid human nose can catch her scent. "Oh!" the selkie says involuntarily. "You're . . ." The woman the artist is cheating on with me. The woman I smell on him, although he claims you're hundreds of miles away.

"Magda Fenton," the woman says. "And you're Dale's new model. Russet, isn't it?"

The selkie nods.

And then a thought seems to strike the woman; she tilts her head to one side, like a bird, and says, "How did you know who I was? Dale showed me his sketches, but he hasn't drawn me in years."

"I smelled you." And then her heart stutters in her chest, because of all the things she shouldn't have said . . .

"You *smelled* me?"

"On him. I'm so sorry."

"He's sleeping with you." She doesn't sound surprised, or even angry. Only tired. "That explains a great deal."

"I really am sorry," the selkie says; she feels sick. Because she can't claim she didn't know the artist was cheating on his wife. She can't even claim she didn't know it mattered. Not when that's why she was sleeping with the artist herself. Because it's the only thing she can do that hurts Byron at all.

"Dale's decisions aren't your fault," the woman says, almost kindly. "But . . . you *smelled* me? How? I don't wear perfume, and I haven't . . . "

The selkie knows she should lie. But she doesn't. She's hurt this woman already, and the woman has not tried to hurt her in return. She has behaved like a sister, not a hunter.

The selkie turns her hands palms up, spreading the fingers.

And she says, "I'm a selkie." It's the first time she's ever spoken the words.

The woman becomes very still for a moment, staring into the selkie's eyes as if she could find truth in them. Then, slowly, she bends her head to look at the selkie's hands, the webs between her fingers, the rough skin of her palms. And then she looks up again, her pale eyes like rock, and says, "Where is your skin?"

The selkie blinks hard against the salt burn of tears. "In there," she says, nodding toward the museum. "Byron hid it in there."

201. Figurehead. Wood. 35" x 20". American, ca. 1850-1860. Figure of a woman, her hands crossed at her breast. Ship unknown.

I believed her.

Dale would have laughed at my gullibility, but I was astonished at how little I cared. I saw the truth, not in her webbed fingers, but in her eyes, which were dark and sad and much older than her face. She was a selkie, a seal-woman, and her soul was trapped in the museum just as the figureheads were.

We walked through the museum together, the only visitors, while she told me about Byron and her skin and in return I told her about the figureheads. Neither one of us mentioned Dale. We didn't go into the figureheads' room, but stopped in front of a diorama, dusty and crude, of an Inuit ice-fishing.

"They're imprisoned," I finished. "Does that seem like nonsense to you?"

"They're man-built things," she said. "I don't see how the ocean can possibly be their home."

"Because they're inanimate?"

"Because men built them," she said with an impatient shrug.

"Not all men are like Byron."

"But you're all . . . " She waved her hand in an angry, inarticulate gesture and said again, "They're man-built things."

"And the works of human beings have no souls?"

"Man-made souls," the selkie said. "Souls that belong with men."

"Souls that would profane your home," I said, understanding.

"You got that right," she muttered, a pitch-perfect imitation of the sullen girl she appeared to be.

There was nothing I could say. I stood silently, helplessly, wondering if it would be worth the effort to try to convince her to come look at the figureheads, or if it would simply be wasted breath. And what, I asked myself, did I think she could do anyway? She was a creature out of a fairytale, but that fairytale had nothing to do with me and my self-proclaimed duty. She had her own problems.

She'd gone from standing hipshot in front of the diorama to leaning on—no, pressing against the glass.

"Russet?" I said.

"My skin," she said, her voice no more than breath and pain. "It's in there."

"In there?" I stared at the mannequin dressed in stiff, moth-eaten sealskins. My double-take was hard enough to hurt.

"How can I get in there?" the selkie said, and I looked away from her yearning hands flattened against the glass.

"There's a door in the back wall, but—" And then I remembered Ezekiel Pitt emerging from a door marked **EMPLOYEES ONLY**. "Come on!"

I wasn't sure she would follow me, but she did. We were halfway down the aisle between the figureheads when she balked, stopping as if she'd been brought up short by an invisible wall. "Are these . . . " I heard her breath catch. "Are these what you were talking about?"

"These are the figureheads, yes."

"I knew I hated Ezekiel Pitt," she said, then shook herself and looked at me, eyes sharp. "Okay, do you have any bright ideas?"

"You mean you—"

"I was wrong, okay?" she said, glaring at me. "I thought you were just, you know, telling stories. It's what you people are good at."

I wasn't sure for a moment who "you people" were. "Don't selkies tell stories?"

"It's not the same. But I *get* it, okay? I'm with the program. Nobody made their souls, and they don't belong here. And you want to help them. I get that, too. And—" She broke off, glowering, daring me to laugh at her. "I didn't think you people cared—didn't think you *could* care, and I was wrong, and I'm sorry. Okay? Now what are we gonna do about it?"

I had an ally, however unwilling and irritated, and I felt some measure of dread lift away from me. "We should start with your skin."

She looked startled, so I elaborated, "We know what to do

there." And then, when her expression didn't change, "I care about that, too."

"Oh." She shook herself and said, brusque efficiency to cover embarrassment: "Yeah, okay. Through here, you think?"

"Unless you'd rather just break the glass," I said, teasing gently, and she responded with a smile as brief and brilliant as a flash of lightning.

"Let's not even get started on what I'd rather do. For now, I'm gonna go with hoping this door isn't locked."

It wasn't. We slunk through it like characters in every bad spy movie I'd ever stayed up watching, long past midnight, instead of trying to sleep in the same bed with Dale. Or with his absence. The hallway was deserted, and the selkie didn't waste any time working her way back along to the diorama's access door.

It wasn't locked, either.

"You realize I can only do this because you're with me," she said. "I mean, I'm scared out of my mind here."

"I wouldn't have thought you'd care about breaking the law."

"I don't. I care about that creepy motherfucker Ezekiel Pitt." She slid into the diorama as smoothly as if the air were water, and was back in ten seconds, shutting the door behind her left-handed; her right hand was clenched white-knuckled in a limp, ratty-looking sealskin.

I knew it was her skin as well as she did; it took my breath away to look at her. Her colors were vivid, her lines clean. She was bright instead of dull, focused instead of blurred. Everything in this town was faded, but not the selkie, not anymore.

"Are you frightened of Ezekiel Pitt now?" I said, curious.

She laughed. It was a strange sound, not merely because she sounded like a seal barking, but because it was so obviously a learned response. "Right now, I'm not afraid of anything," she said. "Let's see what we can do for your figureheads."

Ezekiel Pitt was waiting on the other side of the **EMPLOYEES ONLY** door.

"Byron called me when he couldn't reach you," he said, looking past me to the selkie. I wasn't even sure he'd registered my presence. "In a tizzy as usual. I told him I'd see what I could do about pulling his chestnuts out of the fire." He expected her to be afraid of him. It was in his voice, his posture, the way he looked at her. He knew it was her fear of him that had kept her imprisoned, and he didn't imagine that could change.

"I wouldn't worry about Byron's nuts if I were you," the selkie said and shoved me gently forward into the figureheads' hall. "You have other problems."

"Do I? Seems like you're the one with the problem, miss. All I have to do is call the cops."

"No," the selkie said. She reached out, caught his wrist. And held. He brought his arm up to wrench away, and he couldn't. "You're a greedy man, Ezekiel Pitt. You're holding what doesn't belong to you. And you need to let go."

"You're confusing me with Byron," Ezekiel Pitt said, still trying to wrench free, and still failing. "And I admit Byron should know better than to think he can hold a—"

"No." He stopped talking, his mouth hanging slightly open, and she said, her voice flat and calm, "Let them go."

He didn't try to pretend he didn't know what she was

talking about. "What do you want me to do? Throw them all in the sea? They're valuable, you know, and the museum—"

"The wood isn't what matters. The wood is only what holds them here. Let them go."

Her grip tightened on his wrist. He was whining now, like a neglected dog: "I can't. I don't know how. I don't know what—"

"Yes, you do." She walked over to the green ecstatic-eyed maiden, bringing Ezekiel Pitt with her. She was a wild creature, and the truth of her nature shone through her like sunlight through glass. He was nothing next to her.

She put his hand on the figurehead's forehead. He was whimpering, and the noise was both pathetic and repulsive. The selkie was inexorable. She said, "Let them go home, Ezekiel Pitt." His face twisted—a snarl of fury, a grimace of pain—and he cried out, "Goddamn you, you bitches!" as if he could make even freedom into a curse.

The figureheads were free.

In the silence, the selkie let Ezekiel Pitt go.

He backed away from her, from the figureheads which now were nothing but wood, man-made things without even man-made souls. He was cradling his hand against his chest; his mouth was working, though no sound came out until he was five feet from the selkie, out of her reach, and then he hissed, "I'm calling the police, you . . . you bitch!" He turned and bolted, shouldering past me as if I, too, were inanimate wood.

The selkie looked at me, bright-eyed, gleeful, and said, "Let's get the hell out of here."

181. Figurehead. Wood. 36" x 18". American, ca. 1850. Figure of a woman holding a sword. Ship unknown.

The woman, who is so much more than the artist's wife, comes with the selkie to the beach. The selkie is glad.

They stand together just above the rush and retreat of the tide, and the silence between them is awkward, painful, a human silence.

The selkie can feel her sisters swimming out in the cold sea; she can feel her wooden sisters, too, singing without sound in the darkness of the deeps. Silence with her sisters won't feel like this, won't be wrong.

She says, "You could come with me. If you wanted?" She wants. She wants this woman to be her sister.

The woman blinks, her pale lashes making it look more like a flinch. "I'm a good swimmer, but—"

"The wood isn't what matters," the selkie says.

"You mean . . . "

"Your wooden sisters will welcome you. I'll bring your seal sisters to meet you."

"Am I so trapped?" the woman murmurs. She looks at her hands. "Is this a wooden prison?"

"I didn't mean it like that."

"Dale would agree with you," the woman says, catching the selkie with her pale eyes. "I'm no more than a figurehead to him."

"Dale's an idiot," the selkie snaps, and the woman laughs. "I didn't mean you were trapped. Dale doesn't have your skin. I just meant, if you *wanted* to . . . "

The woman smiles, a smile as warm as a sister's love.

"Thank you. But the ocean isn't my home. It might become my prison."

The selkie nods. She does understand. "You won't go back to Dale, will you?"

"Not a chance," her sister says and laughs, the ecstatic laughter of a child.

"If you ever see Byron, you can tell him from me to fuck off. I'm going home." She strips her clothes off as the sea washes around her feet. Carrying her skin, she wades out up to her waist; then, with one last kick of her human legs, she jack-knifes into the water and clads herself in her true skin. She surfaces fifty yards out, already hearing her sisters' joy, and glances back.

Her sister is standing on the shore, waving good-bye.

Samantha Henderson lives in Southern California with her family. Her fiction and poetry has been published in Realms of Fantasy, Strange Horizons, Chizine, Fantasy Magazine, Weird Tales, *and* Lone Star Stories. *For more information, see her website at* www.samanthahenderson.com

"Shallot"—I always thought of the Lady of Shalott as an alien rather than Elaine of Astolat.

SHALLOT

Samantha Henderson

"Oh—the Lady!"

Little-Ghu stared dreamily across the water at the small, triangular islet with its queer castle, and Michael laughed, chunks of green apple falling from his mouth. The three boys lay on the stubble of the new-mown barley field, watching the river twinkle.

"I saw her fall," offered Cam, although he could not be sure.

"Ha! 'Twas long before your dam was bred that *she* fell. A hundred year ago."

Cam scratched his head. Michael usually had the right of it, but he did have the dim impression of a streak of green like the stories the Friar told of a comet, and the taint of burning air, and the island flaring emerald for a day, and all the sheep dead. But maybe it was the stories the old men told.

"My Da said she's always been here," Michael continued,

"and the star an angel falling to her. He said the King's Men should burn all down, burn all black, and send her back to Hell."

Little-Ghu had not stopped staring across the water. "I saw her eyes, once."

Michael stopped. Little-Ghu was crazy enough to be telling the truth. Little-Ghu could toss fifty bales without sweat and lift a fallen log to rescue a kitten. He was slow to anger and slower of thought; he liked to taste the goat cheese before it was ripe, although his belly hurt each time; he never lied.

"Summer, when the river were low," he went on. "There's a bar down o'er, in the narrows where the boats don' go, and I waded across."

"Strewth!" They were entranced and horrified. They say that those who touch the isle will die of sores and the wasting-sickness. And Big-Ghu would no doubt beat his son if he knew.

"Was she fair as the Queen?" said Cam. It mattered not that none had seen the Queen. They all knew a Queen must, by definition, be fair. Little-Ghu shuddered.

"Her eyes were all I saw, and that was enough. And hair, I think, black and long. I crept to that window, yonder, and looked inside, and she was there. She looked at me, straight on. Huge yes, they were, black as sloes. I think I should go mad if I should see the rest."

"Will ye be her knight then, and go her service?" teased Michael. But Little-Ghu was beyond him, staring at the wall, the parapets.

"The Lady, the Lady," he muttered, all entranced.

Her eyes indeed were large, and dark, and shiny. Little-Ghu was mistaken quite about the hair, for she had none, nor needed none, nor gave it any thought. And she had done more than look at him through the bubbled windows of her chamber, although Little-Ghu remembered it not. He was her man indeed.

Call him back.

They were open, this race, their minds open and smooth, ready to be planted. As the boy crept about the hive she'd sensed him and waited. His face, white and startled and doughy; his mind, white and startled and doughy. It was little effort to hold him there and probe within. How strange that their minds were all in one place, inside their brainmeat, and in no other time but the present. He stared at her, unresisting, as she prodded.

Castle, she understood; she learned it from the brainmeats that foraged about the fields to either side. *Castle* meant stone, and fighting, and the storage of *grain*. Curious, she unraveled the word where it lived inside this boy, and found more— towers, and flags snapping in the breeze, jewels and velvets, proud men on horses. He'd watched it all go by with the taste of green apple on his tongue and the print of his father's belt warm on his back, for malingering. Inside the tangle of *Castle* she found another, *Lady*, and there was a song with this one. Crude and crippled, but a song nonetheless, that wove so deeply within the word *Lady* that she couldn't tease them apart. Here's where the jewels and the velvets lived, and the smell of spice and oranges, and a hand lain for an instant on an armored shoulder. She didn't understand, but the song gave it a form and sense she could taste and ponder.

The boy outside the rough glass was shaking. She searched behind his eye and found the nerve, found the little image of herself, delicate as a wax bubble and tucked it into the word *Lady*. And then she sent him home, primed for her call.

Time to call him back.

All sterile, all. The egg-cradles she had woven in careful tiers from floor to ceiling of her high tower, useless. Their heavy round burdens, naught but shell and fluid. Nothing quickened there. Almost useless to try, anyway, but all she could do, without the Intersect to tup her there; the yolk would rarely quicken without, strange and charmed, another's matter. And the Intersect had failed to meet her here, had diverged so slight, so deadly on the path and as she/shem blazed, safe but lonely, onto the blessed isle he/hem crashed, imploded, out-then-in, toppling *pines, they were, fair tall pines of Russia* in a fragrant burst of balsam, somewhere else entirely, sometime else entirely. Somewhere out of the blossoming river of time, a cry, implosion, then silence. The Intersect was bound to her—they would not send another. They would dismiss this place, this time as flawed and invest resource and breeders elsewhere, only checking here and there to see if she, against odds, had succeeded.

She crashed alone, and while her nets embraced her, the ship that was her/she that was the ship blossomed like a flower and plunged its petals deep into the strange soils, tasting it and grain by grain building her hive, high and hollow, ready for eggs doomed never to quicken, while the four brief seasons of this world faded one to other, green to gold to white to pale green eleven, twenty-two, thirty-three times round.

There was a bare chance they'd ripe on their own, although the offspring were headblind and crippled the line might continue and strengthen. And there were other ways, born of desperation. She would not quit now.

So she called Little-Ghu back to her, and in cooling autumn night he went through the shorn fields, waded-then-swam the swollen waters and dragged himself on her shores, half-drowned. Doors opened for him and closed behind, and the spirits of the air whispered in the frigid air of the castle while he knelt before his Lady.

A hand that was not a hand snaked down to stroke Little-Ghu's cheek. Delicate claws shredded away his tattered shirt and teased away the epidermis, raveled apart the muscle fibers underneath. All the while he was still, drowning in a song of cinnamon and clove, eyes shut tight.

It does not hurt. It does not hurt. I am your Lady.

Planted, one by one, like peas in a hole, tucked between the red and white, fiber and fascia, grain in the furrow, spores on the mud. Naught to do but wait, now, and pray that her germ cells would find something in his to batten on.

Over the hill they rode, following the riverbank, Bedwyr and Cai and Gwalchmai and Caradoc—Lance du Lac brightest of them all, down the river to Camelot, while the autumn sun spilled like a broken yoke over the trees and fields and touched their shoulders with gold. Michael and Cam watched them from the crotch of an ash; Little-Ghu was home, sick. His back was a nightmare of sores and pustules, his sister said, and midwife and priest were called regardless of cost.

"Bedwyr fought the giants of Wales," said Cam. "And killed a dozen. I'm going to run and 'prentice to a squire, I am."

"Will he die?" said Michael, still thinking on Little-Ghu.

"Oh, aye," said Cam, still staring and dreaming of horse and giants and the rolling hills of Wales.

It was the secret pleasure and sin of Padre Thomas to walk past the rim of the green fields, where the wheat blackened sometimes where the island curved: the demon's isle, they called it sometimes. The Demon of Shallot, that some called the Lady, and some *la Belle*. He knew she didn't fall from Heaven. He knew she must be devil-spawn. But she'd been there since he was in bum-rags, and was part of the land's inheritance, was she not? And he must admit, when he walked beside Shallot, he grew accustomed, even desirous of the tickle in his brain, the curious, questing inquiry from that presence.

What strange songs you sing, it—she, perhaps—had said once, halting him in his tracks. *Alpha, and omega, and three-no-four, three-no-four.*

And he'd smiled, then frowned and turned aside, hurrying home, but returned to the path the next day, and let the mind move in his, longing for that strong-thewed tickle.

Three things are never satisfied, she echoed at him. *And one is Sheol, the empty womb.*

The grave, he echoed back, *Sheol is the grave. The grave, the womb, the earth for water, the fire for everything. There are four.*

Three, the demon returned. *Your own song says three.*

From the island, she watched them too, her webs rent about her. The last eggs, those she'd planted with some of the boy's queer proteins, lay with their tops sheared off, their contents inert.

She did not despair. Her race did not despair.

Sheol.

The empty womb.

Years since a boat spun about from upstream and beached at the island, moving up and down with the tides, never enough to break free. She watched it, sometimes, when the waters were high and rain fell and no brainmeats came for days.

Now she gathered a crook-ful of the torn webbing-material and wet it, and spun it, and caressed it, and molded it, and took of herself within it, and presently it was glass-thick and glass-solid, opaque and delicately colored, a mask in the shape of a woman's face, framed by the song in Lance du Lac's head.

The waters were medium-low and calm. Without looking back at the destroyed nest, the dead eggs, she clutched the mask to her and broke her seals; the wall shivered and fell open, and she breathed the outside air at last, heavy and thick with pollen, with the chaff of wheat fields, with the mold of the stream, with the microbes that already were eagerly feeding on her. Quick, quick, there was no time to lose, and she loosened the little boat from its place and spread her silks upon it and, as it bobbed dangerously, lay down with the mask over her face-tendrils, her large gleaming eyes.

The craft bobbed uncertainly, as if reluctant to leave its longtime home, then nosed out into the stream until a current caught it, and it arrowed downstream, and she lay and watched the sky and felt herself decay.

Little-Ghu felt no pain as he lay on his belly on the rough blankets, as Padre Thomas and witch-Mary picked at the boils on his back, which burst open one by one. Small headless creatures coiled within each one, mostly still but some stirred, and these the priest and the midwife crushed, quickly between their thumbs, and dropped into a bucket of vinegar-wine. They had looked at each other, priest and witch, bonded in horror as the little parasites burst forth from the flesh beneath their hands, dozens of little demons.

The islet shall burn, though Thomas as he tried not to listen to the boys tuneless, blissful humming as he lay under their hands. *Tomorrow, it will burn, and the Sheol-thing with it.*

Outside Big-Ghu stood by a great gnarled oak, half-live and half-rotted out. As he heard the priest exclaim once, involuntarily, he struck the pulpy wood with his ham-fist, filling the air with wood-dust and fracturing one of his fingers.

The little boat was caught on the rushes midstream; Lance watched, frowning as it rotated and broke free. It was leaky and floated half-submerged under its burden.

The Court had spilled out, in the warm twilight, to the decking where the water lapped beneath, the women trailing rich fabrics on the rough wood, the men sleepy with wine. Some joined him in watching the derelict bump along the piers, until it came to rest on a snag beneath them and all gasped in wonder at the woman inside, dead and fair as glass. Some of the women, too, came to see, and a dozen songs were hatched in their brainmeats, could but She, Sheol hear them.

Lance crouched low and fit two fingers under the edge of the mask, thinking as he did that he shouldn't, trying to stop his own impulsive movement but he couldn't; he pulled it back as one would tear a scab away from a half-healed wound. He rose and stood, staring, the mask dangling from his hand and it seemed to those who stood a ways back that Lance du Lac, the perfect knight, had torn the very face from a beautiful lady. And then the mask fell from his fingers and shattered on the decking.

One fragment spun away and came to rest at the feet of the Queen where she stood at the lip of the doorway—a staring glass eye and the start of the curve of the bridge of the nose. The broken edge glinted sharp and harsh, the surface was matte and crushed with something clear and viscous. The Queen shuddered and stepped back. Most rare, puissant, noble, false-called the perfect knight. Love turned fetid in her throat—she hated him now. A horrid kind of pity, a sister-feeling blossomed in her for a moment, and then she kicked the fragment away with an embroidered slipper and fled inside.

Lance looked down into liquid horror; what remained of features that had never been human were rapidly dissolving into a pool that settled in the bottom of the sinking boat. As the bilge overcame there was a tiny *pop*, a burst of spores that blossomed over the surface, and never reached the decking— ineffective, they fell back against the water, speckling it like pollen. Far away, Padre Thomas wept and did not know why, and the small slimy thing in his palm convulsed and moved no more.

Later, when the boat had sunk to bottom and only a rotted plank and a greasy swirl remained on the surface, none was left to see: inside the hall there was dancing and the blaze of candles to make the women's gowns more golden than before, and the gems to shine like fire.

Maura McHugh lives in Galway, Ireland, where neolithic graves moulder in the shadow of skeletal communication masts. She writes the mutated fiction of her dreams across all media. Her website is: splinister. com "Bone Mother" arose from a simple "what if?" question, and once asked, the protagonist supplied all the answers.

BONE MOTHER

Maura McHugh

The house tilted. A thighbone rolled off my kitchen table and clattered onto the floorboards. I cocked my head and waited for a warning. Silence. It was still sulking.

I whacked its bony walls with my hawthorn stick. "Out with it!" I said.

"A man approaches, you withered old crone!" The floor trembled with irritation.

"A fine house you are! Allowing a stranger to sneak up on me."

I pulled tangles back from my ears, which set off the rat skulls knotted into my hair. A tap from my stick shut their jawbones. The jingle of a horse's reins drifted through the half-open window.

I knocked my walking stick against the rafter fashioned from a mammoth tusk, carved with runes. All activity ceased. My servants—three pairs of disembodied hands—hung in the air above the table, paused in their task of sorting the stack

61

of bones into animal or human. The spiders that infested the thatch stopped in mid-spin. Cobwebbed chains of nails and bundles of herbs swayed from the beam. The only sound was the breathing of the redbrick oven. It huffed out a ball of disgruntled smoke: "Ouch!"

I scuttled to the window, and propped my dugs on the sill as I leaned out to get a gander at the fellow. Despite the lingering sting of that morning's quarrel, I trusted the house to shield me from his eyes.

From my vantage point I should have had a fine view across the compound, past the skeleton fence, and into the breathless gap between the forest and my home, but my weak eyes only saw a blurred outline of a man on a horse leading a pack animal.

My long nose twitched. It makes drinking from small cups inconvenient, but I can smell yesterday's fart, and last night's nightmare. I sniffed. "Mud from the mountains weighs his cloak. It was woven from wool in," I inhaled again, "Moldavia. Underneath the sweat, and the reek of blood and death, is a memory of . . . cloves and cinnamon."

"Can I eat him?" the house whined. I caressed its bleached-white walls, and it leaned into my touch. The fire sighed.

"Cross your gutters that he doesn't know the charm," I said, and squinted for better sight.

The man halted at the gate, and glanced upwards, but the hood drowned his face in shadow. There wasn't a whiff of fear from him at the sight of the gateposts topped with glowing skulls. Leather creaked, and he rose in his stirrups. He brandished a wand that stank of borrowed magic.

The man wove a glyph in the air and I leaned back, wary.

The sigil flashed like sparks from a smithy's fire. Even I could see it. My knuckles cracked as I tightened my grip on the window.

"House of Bone, lower your legs and rest. Gate of Skulls, admit this guest," he said.

"He knows it!" the house moaned. Its giant chicken legs creaked and the floor bobbed as it shuffled around so the front door faced the gate. It eased downwards.

"I haven't heard that version since the plague," I muttered, and slammed the window shut. With a snap of my fingers the hands sprang into action and tidied the bones into the oak chest where I kept leftovers. They blinked out of existence at another click. I picked up a file and sawed at my iron teeth for a moment. With the tip of my tongue I tested its edge—nice and sharp. I lowered myself almost double, and clawed at my hair so the matted weave trailed after me.

"Ow! Ow! Ow!" said the rat skulls as they clacked off the floor.

The house crashed into the ground, and I grabbed a wall to steady myself. I poked it in the ribs. Smoke belched from the fire as an apology.

The door swung open. The man had dismounted and thrown back his cloak over one shoulder to reveal a pleated tight-fitting jacket, leggings, and splattered riding boots. His right hand flirted with his sword hilt, which smelled of Spain, hot fires, and whetstones.

I grovelled low. "Can I help you, my lord?"

"I doubt it, hag," he said. I stabbed my stick into the dirt path instead of skewering his eyeballs. "I seek the bone witch." He peeled off his gloves, and peered past my hunched back into the room beyond. His accent had a Wallachian base, with a Turkish flourish.

"Who wishes an audience with the Mistress of Bones?"

"Vladislav Basarab."

His ancestry sang in his name: ruthless and stubborn rulers of southern Transylvania. I saw the native Dacians of his lineage surge on horses against the invading Romans, then the Pechenegs, and later the Mongols, but most recently the Turks. His was a pedigree of resistance, and tyranny.

I unfolded myself slowly until my head brushed the lintel. He stepped back, and looked up. Wet black hair slicked his high cheekbones, but the twin dark wells of his eyes reflected nothing.

"Baba Yaga bids you welcome, young Vladislav, son of the Dragon." The rat skulls chittered my praise. "Do you come of your own free will, or did someone send you?" The house leaned in to hear his response. The wrong answer would grant us a meal.

From under his cloak he produced a blue rose.

How had I not sensed it?

I tasted the peppery tang of cunning magic I had thought forgotten in Christian lands. My eyelids lowered at the flower's intoxicating scent. It promised porcelain skin, clear eyes, and an end to aching joints. All I could see were the sky-blue petals that curled away from an indigo centre.

As if from a distance I heard his answer.

"I come to trade, Bone Mother, for the secrets of life and death."

The souls of the damned trapped in my house's walls screeched their frustration.

The flower lay on the table, and its perfume lulled me. It conjured memories: sienna eyes under copper hair; a spurned hand; a drop of blood, and the pact of Guardianship, which brought long life in a decaying shell.

I blinked the past away and did not stare at the rose, despite my desire. The infrequent potions I concocted from its petals were all that revived my body. When last I'd tasted its ambrosia Alexander had held Constantinople.

I summoned my servants, and at least Vladislav started in surprise as one wizened hand wielded a poker on the embers while the other held open the oven's door. The other two pairs bore blue-patterned china plates and wide navy glasses to the table.

Vladislav shrugged off his cloak on the back of a big chair with arms made of wolf's ribcages, and a seat covered in cured pygmy skins. He settled into it, comfortable, and stroked the curving bone. I perched on the three-legged stool made from Minotaur horns.

He leaned down, pulled a bottle of kvass from a greasy saddlebag, and placed it on the table. He was irritatingly well prepared.

"Where did you find the rose?" I snapped.

"My mother's people are from Moldavia." He picked up the rose by its black stem and twirled it slowly; the thorns had an evil curved point. "Some of them remember our heretical past." He laid it upon the table a little closer to me.

"You imperil your soul with such devilry." I restrained a smirk.

"The Lord guides my path. He delivered me from the Turks, and urges me to build a strong Wallachia."

I nodded at one pair of hands and they poured kvass into the containers. "I understand your younger brother, Radu, enjoyed Turkish company. The Sultan's in particular."

Vladislav's knuckles whitened as he gripped the glass. If he broke it I'd fillet him like a trout, and damn the rules of hospitality.

"Maybe he was wise to spurn women. They offer little beyond a dowry and heirs."

Once I'd stopped a man's heart with a glance, but his eyes did not flinch from my gaze. I grabbed my tits and gazed down at them. "Yes, still a woman." He pulled back in disgust. I leaned forward and hissed, "Still a witch."

"The lord protects me from your wickedness," and his hand crept to the crucifix around his neck.

"To faith," I said, "however misguided," and knocked back the kvass. I smacked my lips as he swallowed the alcohol in one gulp. "Is your father well?" I asked, hoping for a lie, and a way to break peace. I dug my nails into the palms of my hands and glanced again at the flower, luminous in the candlelight. I had smelled his father's bones wrapped up in elk's leather on the back of Vladislav's mule.

"Slaughtered, by Hunyadi's army. Along with my mother." He paused and turned the glass in his hand so the light spun a shower of navy stars across the table and the rose. I smelled blood as my nails punctured my skin. "They buried my brother alive. I never found his grave."

"I heard you were routed from the capital, and ran to Bogdan of Moldavia squealing for sanctuary." I gave him a good view of my iron teeth as I smiled.

The glass vibrated when he banged it on the table. "I will take Tirgoviste again."

I gestured towards the rose. "What's your price?"

"I need the advice of my father to regain the throne."

I waited.

He moved the flower again, almost within my reach. "You are the Guardian of the waters of life and death," he said, "It lies within your power to resurrect him."

"The flower's not worth necromancy." I was lying. "Mourn your family, marry, have children, and teach them to fight. There are always Turks and Christians to slaughter."

"Were you ever beautiful, witch?" His tone was cold like the earth under ice. "How many wrinkles could this flower erase?"

It was so close.

A sliver of brown edged a cerulean petal. He'd removed the charm that kept it fresh. Now it rotted slowly. I only had a couple of days.

"If you take it by force it will turn to ash instantly," he whispered.

The spicy taste of a spell lingered. Something akin to admiration sparked in me, or maybe it was fury. I've always had difficulty telling them apart.

"I have to gather the waters."

He nodded. "Tomorrow, then."

"You sleep in the barn," I added, "if you want to pass the night unmolested." He grimaced at my leer.

I woke to the sound of the hands reviving the fire, and laying out food. I crunched the shells of the eggs they left me for breakfast, and sucked the wriggling embryos in one go. After some grumbling, the house lowered itself to the ground.

"Just kill him, Bone Mother," it said as it hit the earth, hard. "And feed his bones to my fire." The flames capered.

I stretched out my hand and my birch broom swept into it. "He has the rose," I said. "Keep locked up tight, and high above the ground." I looked at my hands, gnarled with pain, and imagined them smooth. "Besides, who says I can't have him *after* I get the flower?"

The door creaked open and I inhaled the scent of clouds boiling over the snow-capped Făgăraş Mountains, a fox ripping into a hare's flesh, and the sweat of the young man who leaned against the doorway of my barn. Straw stuck to his clothes. "After all," I said, "when I'm younger again, I'll have needs."

I whistled, and from inside the barn Vlad's horse screamed and the mule kicked the walls. He turned, and leaped out of the path of my huge iron mortar, which whizzed past him and across the ground to hover beside me. Aware of his appraising gaze I jumped inside the mortar's bowl and showed no trace of the pain the impact caused. I brandished the long pine pestle in my right hand. There was wonder on his face, and he smelled of excitement, but not fear.

I frowned. "I'll expect payment when I return, *voivode*."

I cracked the pestle against the ancient iron, and the mortar climbed towards the sky. The ground beneath quaked, and the trees around the compound bent and shook like they were whipped by fierce winds. The house straightened its legs and rose as I drifted upwards. I shrieked, urging the mortar across forests and rivers, and swept away my trail with the broom. My hair streamed after me, and the rat skulls sang of dead cats and dunghills.

I returned to my compound at twilight, exhausted. Each time the trip took longer, but I could almost taste the honeyed infusion of blue petals on my tongue. The earth shuddered, and the trees flailed as the mortar eased downwards. The house squatted on the ground. The door was open, and no smoke breathed from the chimney.

I hopped out of the mortar, dropped the pestle and broom to the ground, gripped the skins of water to my chest, and hobbled on my walking stick to the doorway.

My house was in disarray. Bloodied fingers from my servants lay scattered on the floor, the door to the stove was open, and the fire was dead.

A lone blue petal stirred amid the ashes scattered before the hearth, and the charred end of a rose stem lay in the cold oven. The hawthorn fell from my grip to the floorboards. A fingerless palm lay in the centre of the table, impaled by a dagger. Soot streaked the walls.

He'd tried to burn my home. I glanced up. The runes of making on the mammoth tusk were intact. Mundane fire wasn't enough. Fury trembled my limbs.

"Mother!" my house babbled between cries, "He made me. I'm sorry! I told him where to go. I told him the source, from where the rivers spring."

I picked up the petal between thumb and forefinger. If I was careful, and brewed the potion well, it was good for a thimbleful: enough to ease the pain for fifty years, and to remind me of youth but not grant it. The process would take a week, and Vladislav would be gone.

Fatigue gnawed my body. "Why did you let him in?"

"I was so hungry, and he had bones!"

I leaned my forehead against a wall and stroked its filthy surface. My hand shook. Eventually hate and age weighed me down onto the stool as my house retold the story of its ordeal.

If I was careful . . .

I gathered twigs and paper, and muttered the charm that lit its flame, even though it cost me strength. Gently, I fed the fire with logs after it caught and burned.

"He is mad," the house whispered, and it puffed angry dark smoke.

"He has a mission," I said.

My home stank of fear and surrender. It was ravenous, and I needed servants.

I brushed the soft petal against my dry cheek and inhaled its perfume. It promised pain-free years to hunt for another rose.

If I was careful . . .

I was the Guardian of the waters of life and death. None could drink them without my permission.

I slipped the petal under my tongue. Saliva flooded my mouth at its sweet taste.

Strength returned, and I rose to my full height. I uncurled my hands and remembered my power. The rat skulls rattled like ivory dice.

The petal dissolved in my mouth.

Through the open door I stared at the night sky. The moon was the shape of an ox skull's horns.

I would spear the Wallachian prince upon them. I would girdle my home with his entrails and wash its walls with his pulp.

I bounded from the house, and leaped high as a mountain goat into the mortar as it rose at my command. The door to my house slammed shut and its legs quivered as it heaved the structure from the ground. Vladislav would pay for that weakness.

I struck the pestle against the side of my mortar and it was a roll of thunder. The iron bowl thrust into the sky.

I shrieked my displeasure and every living being within earshot fell to the ground and pissed itself in fear.

He had already drunk from the stream of life by the time I arrived.

Trees snapped and broke under the force of my fury as I landed in the clearing before the cave. I hurtled from the mortar before it landed, and rock cracked underneath my boots.

Vladislav waited at the entrance, resplendent in armour. Charms etched into his breastplate glowed, and old enchantments misted his drawn sword blade. His belief had not stopped him thieving spells from the mountain folk who had gleaned their tricks from water, earth, and air. I had been the midwife of such magic.

"I am now immortal, *old woman*." Vladislav's voice rang with faith and arrogance. "I am the instrument of righteousness. I shall crush the unfaithful, guide the humble . . . "

I snapped my fingers and the blade tore from his grasp and embedded hilt-first in a boulder of granite. Its edge shone in the light of the moon's horns. I clapped my hands and his breastplate fell apart and clanked on the ground.

Yet he crouched and grinned as I rushed towards him, my hands spread wide, my nails sharp, and my teeth bared.

"Come on," he goaded, and the crucifix around his neck glinted.

I punched him, broke his thin nose, and he flew back into the rock wall and his ribs shattered. He spat blood from his mouth, but did not moan. His dark eyes were wells of brutality. Within them I spied years of torture, and a glacial promise forged in a Turkish prison: he would visit horror upon any who caused him pain—family, ally, or ancient foe.

I seized the front of his tunic and threw him upon his sword. It impaled his chest. It was excruciating, but he would not die. Not now. Immortality kept him from death, but not from suffering, or decay. I knew the cost well.

He lay on the ground, the sword skewered through his broken chest, and blood splattered on his face. Yet he laughed . . . choked . . . sneered.

"You'll dry up like dust, witch. No rose will restore your bloom."

The sugary taste faded. I stood above him, and uncapped one of the skins. I reached down, squeezed his jaws, and pried them open.

I poured the waters of death into his mouth, and watched his eyes widen as he sensed the change. His wounds healed, the blood flow ceased, and his heart stopped. I hunkered down beside him, my bony knees level with my ears, as he flopped like a landed fish.

"You are alive, Vladislav, but you are also dead. You will

thirst for blood, but it will never satisfy you. Your victims will be legion, and my house and I will feed upon their corpses. You will drive your enemies from your land, but you will never know peace, or redemption."

I pulled him from his sword, and threw him across the clearing. Flesh sizzled, and Vladislav's limp hands scrabbled at his neck. He ripped the crucifix off and threw it to the ground.

I grinned. "Only the sun will unravel this spell." The prince shuddered, and gasped as he died and the red thirst gripped him. I reached down and ripped a chunk of hair from his scalp. He screamed and bared his teeth. They had a new sharpness. I showed him the bloody hank before I tucked it into a pocket. "My revenge upon you will be long in coming, and complete." The sweetness died in my mouth.

He attempted to rise, and failed.

I hid my limp as I walked to the mortar, and climbed carefully into its basin.

With a strike of the pestle the mortar ascended into darkness, and I did not look back.

I sowed Vladislav's hair into a hexing doll to keep track of him over the years. Whenever my house and I were hungry I'd ask it where Vladislav had last visited. It would pull its awkward woollen body upright, and point its crude hand towards bloodshed.

Vlad the Impaler massacred thousands while he dined on foods that never nourished him, and consorted with women who never pleased him. He delivered misery and terror in his drive to slack an endless appetite.

We feasted well during his reign. Always, I hunted for a blue rose, but it eluded me.

One night, as I whipped my mortar through the air I sensed a change in the hexing doll, which I kept in my pocket. It raised a limp arm. I followed its signs until I crossed the Danube, and traversed the lands of the Ottoman Empire where the white turbaned men shrank from my shadow. After a tiring journey the doll drew me to a city of spires, minarets, and gold domes, where prayers rang out as the sky pinked for the dawn. The scent of cloves and cinnamon wafted upwards. There I found him, or what was left.

His head was stuck upon a spear, the spine and throat ragged and hinting at a long and torturous decapitation. I dropped the hexing doll, and watched it land with a spray of sparks in a charcoal brazier far below. I flew close so my failing sight could behold his death.

His eyelids fluttered open, and the thirst continued to rage in his eyes.

I smiled, baring my iron teeth. The muscles around his lips twitched into a rictus.

The first rays of sunlight touched his face, and seared it black. His mouth opened, but whether it was to howl, or laugh, I did not know.

As his eyes boiled I thought of the luminous blue flower, and the beauty he'd stolen from me. He'd gotten off easy.

I clacked pine against iron, and urged the mortar upwards. Sluggish, it lifted above the clouds, where my passing would go unnoticed. I slumped against the cold metal. The pestle and broom were heavy in my aged hands.

In the airless cerulean expanse, I tasted a burst of nectar.

My movements were fluid, and painless. The far mountains and forests of my birthplace sharpened and became clear.

I smelled gore from a recent battlefield far beneath me; fresh food for the pot. The rat skulls chattered nonsense. I floated towards home.

Lisa Mantchev casts her spells from an ancient tree in the Pacific Northwest. When not scribbling, she is by turns an earth elemental, English professor, actress, artist, dog wrangler, mommy, and domestic goddess. Her stories have been published in places like Strange Horizons and New Voices in Science Fiction, and she has stories slated to appear in Weird Tales, Electric Velocipede and various anthologies. She has just completed her first novel, entitled Scrimshaw. You can Taste the Bad Candy at her website: www.lisamantchev.com

"The Greats Come A-Callin'" is as near and dear to my heart as a story can be. The Aunts really existed, as did their mother, Addie Mae. The family farmstead, constructed of bricks that were carted by the wagonload more than sixty miles, still stands in Northern California. But no one knows what happened to the bunny cookie cutter.

THE GREATS COME A-CALLIN'

Lisa Mantchev

"Not one of those new-fangled electric monstrosities," Great Great Aunt Mabel said from the depths of my handbag, somewhere between the Tic Tacs and a dry cleaning receipt. "A treadle is the only way to go if you want to have any control over your fabric."

"But I don't want a sewing machine." I hitched my purse up my arm, fighting the weight of the brick inside. "I don't need it and I don't have room for it. I don't know how to sew, for Christ's sake, much less on a rusty old Singer."

"Don't take the name of the Lord in vain, my miss." That was my Great Great Grandmother Addie Mae, but I wasn't having any of her sass.

"Oh please. We're Methodists. That's like Presbyterian Lite." I backed out of the fabric store wondering where the heck I was going to find a treadle sewing machine. "Why couldn't Meemaw have sent me a freaking knickknack instead of all y'all?"

When my grandparents decided to sell the family farmhouse and retire, they sorted through a hundred years of dust and memories stored in the basement and attic. They sent my sister a set of Fostoria crystal and the secret recipe for chicken and dumplings. My cousin got the player piano and the crumbling rolls of music, a cascade of notes spilling from the slit in the wheezing cardboard box. They divvied up furniture, record albums, vintage Barbie dolls and Depression glass.

"We're sending you a box, Elizabeth. Keep an eye out for the mailman," my grandmother said. Meemaw was the only one that ever called me Elizabeth; to everyone else I was Lizbit or that up-and-coming artist Miss Greene. My family name tied me to summers at their house, cranking the ice cream churn until my arm about fell off, running through corn that grew taller than my head and snapping green beans by the bowlful.

"As long as it's not Great Great Aunt Olive's fox fur stole," I told her, the phone cradled between my ear and my shoulder as I hot-glued feathers to the angel perched on my canvas.

"That thing still had its head attached and its eyeballs creeped me out."

"It's not the stole. One of the church ladies wanted that." An Alabama-twang crawled into her voice, like they'd already pulled up stakes and left. A hollow ache filled my chest; I'd never worried about going "home," but now some upstart city woman owned our property and was all talk about jazz festivals in the barn and rotational organic farming.

"Is it the bunny cookie cutter?" I rummaged in a plastic bin in search of more beads.

Meemaw laughed. "I haven't thought about that thing in years. I haven't seen it since Mabel passed."

I sent a wistful thought after the procession of bunny sugar cookies that marched across the yellow Formica table each Easter of my childhood.

"Well, damn. If you come across it, let me know."

"I'll do that, hon. But when's the last time you baked anything?"

Meemaw would not consider prepackaged break-apart cookies baking; baking involved buttermilk and biscuit dough, lard if you could get it and shortening if you couldn't.

"It's been a while," I admitted, suddenly hungry for an egg fried in butter, toast with homemade jam and about a pound of bacon. Maybe a coconut pound cake with powdered sugar glaze (Twice Great Aunt Mabel's recipe). And a batch of cream caramels (her sister, Elva's).

Matriarch extraordinaire Addie Mae had raised a passel of girls. Everyone said I looked just like the original Elizabeth, but she'd died before I was born. All I had for comparison was an ancient black and white photo of all the girls in front of the brick farmhouse, squinting at the camera and solemn-faced.

"Well, I'll let you get back to your work." I heard a tinge of regret in Meemaw's voice as well; she'd painted watercolors and oils before the arthritis twisted her fingers into knots. "Love you, darlin'."

"Love you, too."

I spent the next several days lost in the haze of a mixed media commission (rhinestones as big as my thumbnail, newspaper clippings and sunshine-yellow acrylic entitled "Good Morning") and barely remembered to eat before I dragged my sorry ass to bed for a few hours sleep.

The day the box arrived, I had a check on the counter with a satisfactory number of zeros in the amount box. My studio was a wreck and there was no food in the house save stale Cheerios and some milk well on its way to becoming yogurt.

"Sign here, please." The mailman looked askance at my Chinese robe, wild bed-head and crusty eyes. I scrawled a haphazard signature on the indicated line and accepted the box.

Smaller than what I'd expected. I sighed over the unvoiced hope of Fiestaware pitchers and went to retrieve the scissors. Meemaw must have used an entire roll of packing tape to seal the box shut. I sawed through the top and unrolled ten yards of bubble wrap and tossed aside a four-foot length of protective packing material to reveal a brick. *Heavy, for its size. And rectangular. Maybe a jewelry box? But I didn't remember a jewelry box.* I stared at it, and the hamster in my brain scampered madly on its wheel as I tried to process my bizarre inheritance.

"What the fuck?" was all the hamster came up with.

"Watch your language, young lady. Profanity makes one sound ignorant and common." Addie Mae wagged her finger at me in admonishment. All I could do was stare, brick in hand, as she examined me and then my kitchen. It was like looking at her black and white photograph in a hazy mirror. "You live in this filth?" She swiped a finger over my long-neglected stove and wrinkled her nose, my nose, the mirror image of my nose on her face.

"I've been busy. I had a commission due, and there's a gallery show coming up." The brick got progressively lighter as the kitchen filled with clucking female forms.

"Shameful," said another. She was a thin wisp of a woman in a flower print dress and sassy hat cocked over one eye. I barely recognized her; Geneva had passed when I was three or four. But Mabel—

"She looks like she could use a decent meal or three." Mabel grinned at me from her perch on my 'filthy' counter. Same elfin face, a mouth meant for laughter and the capable hands I remembered encrusted with dirt from the garden until she fell asleep amongst the roses in her ninety-sixth year.

"We're going to need supplies," said Elva, "for cleaning and cooking. And I doubt she has a sewing machine."

"Why would I need a sewing machine? I don't *sew*!"

The aunts and their mother talked over, around and on top of me. Their chatter buzzed in my ears like bee song; it was making me dizzy. Mabel hopped off the counter and patted my arm in a gesture soft as a swirl of dandelion down.

"To sew on, silly." She faded away and the brick grew heavy with the weight of her. "Don't forget to put on some lipstick before we go out. You look like death."

Mabel sat at the sewing machine for hours the first day, sewing aprons from my memory. I must have watched her whip together hundreds of them over the years, for church bazaars and fundraisers. Flower-print calico draped every chair. Rickrack zigzagged over my counters; counters that gleamed with an unfamiliar polish.

The Aunts and their mama insisted on a vicious spring cleaning, even when I pointed out it was June. They worked domestic magic on the windows and floors. The kitchen smelled like yeast and Sunday roast, even on Tuesday.

I took refuge in my studio. The Aunts made their presence felt even there, with vases of flowers tucked in the corners and a feather duster flicked over me when I'd sat too long, in their opinion.

With my last piece for the show completed (a composite of papier-mâché, leather fringe and stained glass entitled "Hop Over the Reservation Fence") I stumbled out of the studio in search of sustenance.

"Hold on a sec, hon." Mabel flapped a flour-sack dishcloth in my general direction. "I have a pie ready to come out of the oven."

Weird. The stove was a top-of-the-line restaurant grade behemoth, but it smelled like wood smoke. And it had been polished within an inch of its stainless steel existence.

"What kind?" I slid into a chair and tried not to look like a pup begging for scraps.

"Apple slice with lemon glaze, just how you like it." She plonked a piece down in front of me without missing a beat, sticking two loaves of bread in the newly vacated oven and stirring a steaming pot on the stovetop. "You want some ice cream with that, sugar?"

"Yes, please." I swallowed a mouthful of drool, not daring to hope—

It *was* vanilla, just like we made all those summers on the porch. Yellow with egg yolks and flecked with brown bits of bean.

"Where is everyone?" I said through a mouthful of sin.

"Elva and Geneva are in the conservatory—"

"What conservatory?" I paused with the spoon mid-way to my mouth.

"The one on the third floor." Mabel checked the contents of a cast-iron pot, a pot that certainly didn't belong to me. "Mama and Olive are doing the wash."

"Wait, go back. I don't have a third floor." I stood up and headed for the back stairs, only to trip on a wooden hutch full of dishes that I didn't know would be there. I hopped on one foot and jabbed at it with my finger. "And where did this come from?"

"Don't be silly, that's always been there," Mabel said as she tasted the contents of her pot and made a face. "This needs something. Keep an eye on it, will you, while I get some herbs?"

"Herbs?" My garden was nothing more than a tangle of crab grass and dandelions run rampant. I followed her out the backdoor, past a row of cooling pies (who was going to eat all of those?!) and into the yard where I froze. The picket fence had been whitewashed, the hedges trimmed back. Roses bloomed in teacup clusters of gold and apricot. Lavender peeked around purple corners. Fourteen aprons flapped in the breeze in defiance of the electric dryer on the sun porch.

"A little sage, I think. And a handful of thyme." Twist and snap; their scent was foreign and familiar all at once.

"You guys have been busy." I rubbed a paint-spattered hand over my face. I must have spent longer in the studio than I thought. Time enough for all of this to grow. Time enough for furniture to be added and a shelf to be built just for pies, for a conservatory to appear on my non-existent third floor, for that first brick Meemaw sent me to go forth and multiply by the thousands; red stone crawled over clapboards and a tendril of ivy reached for the windowsill. Before long, it would crawl all the way to the roof.

Someone upstairs had opened the windows and musical notes drifted over us like milkweed. My arms broke out in goose flesh.

"Who's doing that? Is it a record player?"

"It's the church band, Elizabeth. You invited them."

Elizabeth. My great-grandmother and the only one of the sisters I hadn't seen yet. A cold wind snaked through the laundry drying on the line and I shivered.

Mabel linked her arm though mine and left a smear of green around my elbow. "Come on, honey. You look like you could use a nice glass of lemonade. And the ice cream must be melting on your pie."

I nearly broke my neck coming down the back stairs to the kitchen the next morning; bleary-eyed, I missed an unexpected twist to the right and the last step was only half as tall as the rest. I bounced off a wall and narrowly missed landing on my head. The sharp pain in my shoulder did a better job of waking me up than a triple espresso.

Stupid house that was changing right under my feet.

Stupid rooster, waking me up.

Stupid Tuesday mornings.

The kitchen was deserted; no doubt the aunts had been up since dawn when the stupid rooster started crowing. I was going to kill him. I'd never killed a chicken, but there was a first time for everything. Wring its neck or take a hatchet to it. But not until I had some coffee in me.

I went to pour it in my jumbo ceramic mug but couldn't find it. All the dishes had been rearranged and they weren't my dishes, anyway. The mismatched crockery mishmash had disappeared, along with most of my "unacceptable" furniture. But I had really liked that mug. I rummaged in the cupboards until I found something that would have to do.

Cupping my bowl of coffee, I shuffled to where the door to my studio should have been and ran into the wall again. Scalding heat flooded down the front of my bathrobe. The bowl hit the floor and detonated in a spectacular explosion.

I stared at the wall, coffee cooling in my cleavage. The hamster in my brain tripped on the wheel and whirled around and around until he fell off and yakked his little hamster guts out. I ran my hand over the wall. No door. Nothing but flower-speckled wallpaper and whitewashed beadboard. I left the mess cooling on the floor and stormed down the hall.

"What happened to my studio?"

All the aunts looked up. Addie Mae clucked her tongue at me. "There's no need to raise your voice, honey."

"Yes, there most certainly is a need to raise my voice." I

advanced on them, finger held like a threat in their general direction. They made quite a picture, gathered in the sitting room-formerly-a-junk hole. Needlepoint, hooked rug, paper pattern in hand, they considered my outburst with quiet tolerance.

"My studio is gone. Gone! As in, vanished. Poof! GONE." I stamped my foot.

"What did you get on your pretty robe?" Mabel fluttered around me. "I just finished sewing that."

I made a mad grab for her hands. "Did you hear me? I want my studio back right now, goddamnit!"

"Elizabeth, now dare you take the Lord's name in vain?"

All the blood drained out of my head. "I'm not Elizabeth," I managed just before I hit the floor. I made bleary return to the world as Addie Mae smacked me on one cheek. A circle of Greats had gathered overhead.

"There, there, dear. Did you have any breakfast this morning? Perhaps you need food." Addie Mae levered me up and as one they towed me to the kitchen.

"The last thing I need right now is more food. None of my pants fit." It hurt to glare, but I managed. "I want it back."

"Your breakfast?"

"My studio!" I shouldn't have yelled. The extra decibels were a hatchet to my head. "All my work for the show was in there."

Six identical expressions: puzzled concern and amused tolerance of artistic eccentricity. "I'm sure we can find you a corner to paint, dear." Addie settled the matter with a firm nod and reached for her skillets.

"I don't want a corner." I rested my head against the table

even as they set silverware around my elbows. "This is my house. I couldn't even find my coffee mug this morning."

"So you poured the coffee on yourself?"

"No, I poured it—" I jerked my thumb where I'd crashed into the wall, but the mess had been dispatched. I hadn't seen anyone touch a mop or a rag. The hamster twitched. Another pulse of pain just behind my left eye. "I have a show this weekend. All the pieces were in the studio."

Again, the exchanged poor-deluded-darling look. "They must be here somewhere." Addie sliced bread with ruthless efficiency. "Perhaps the basement?"

"The damp would hardly be good for them down there." Mabel opened the door to the pantry and selected a jar of golden peaches. Sunlight glimmered on the surface of a thousand glass jars; the rainbow promise of a summer's harvest of produce. "With the creek and all."

I wanted to shout "what basement?!" but I was out of exclamation points.

You're not Elizabeth, I told the hamster.

But the hamster had succumbed to a diabetic coma, his little furry mouth ringed with—what else?—pie.

I waited for a quiet moment (in between pitting cherries and pinching back the marigold heads) to sneak down to the basement. The third stair no longer creaked, no doubt pounded into silent submission by one of the sisters; otherwise it seemed much the same. But the paintings weren't there. All I found were countless tubs filled with butter and covered with damp dishtowels; enough saturated fat to kill several armies through the cunning use of cholesterol. I was afraid to wonder where they were stowing the cows.

The creek required further investigation, but then I nearly stepped in it. It bubbled up in one corner and snaked a faintly sulfurous path across the floor. I filled a metal dipper and sipped from it while sitting on an upturned milk pail.

"Did you find them?" Mabel called down the stairs.

"No, they're not here."

"We checked the attic. Nothing there but trunks of quilts and dried herbs."

"Great. I'm sure my agent will be thrilled by a rack of moldering quilts next to a display of jam pots." I stuck my finger in a pan of cream, knowing full well I'd catch hell for it later, but willing to take my chances with Addie Mae.

"If Addie sees you doing that, your backside will be in a whole world of hurt."

"I have no idea what you're talking about!" I smoothed the cream over as best I could, then stood on tiptoe to put it back on the shelf.

"Are you coming up? The minister is coming to supper, and I could use some help setting the table."

I turned to holler something rude in retort, but another figure stood between me and the stairs; faded by the half-light and as familiar to me as my own face.

"So I do look like you." The cheekbones were slightly higher, the nose more aquiline. "Why have you been hiding?"

"I died before you were born, so you can't remember me." She tilted her head to one side. "My, it's odd to see you like this. I had a daughter—"

"Who had a daughter, who had me." I studied her, wondered a thousand things. Wondered what kind of pie she liked best.

"Imagine that." She searched for something in my face she couldn't find. "The others are starting to think that you're me."

"I guess there's only room in the house for one Elizabeth at a time." I felt ashamed, like I'd stolen her rightful place although I hadn't done anything of the sort. "I didn't mean to. It just happened . . . started with that stupid brick. Now I wish it *had* been Aunt Olive's stupid fox fur."

"That thing was hideous. I always hated it." Elizabeth shuddered. "The girls will run right over the top of you if you let them. And you mustn't let them."

"Seems too late to do anything about it now." I scrubbed my face with one hand. "I don't suppose you know what happened to my paintings? My studio."

She shook her head. "No, we never had a studio. Unless—"

"Unless what?" Even in the semi-darkness, I could see the flush crawl across her cheeks.

"I used to do a little painting. Now and then."

I couldn't help but bounce. "Where?"

"Out in the hayloft."

"Hayloft." I blinked. "In the barn? But we don't have a barn."

It was her turn to blink. "You don't?"

"No." I thought it over. "At least, we don't have a barn yet."

"Oh really?" She had a dimple just like mine when she smiled. "And just how soon do you think you can rustle up a barn?"

"No time at all, I think." I stood up and righted the milk pail. "They have to be hiding the cows somewhere."

"We need to have a barn." I rolled out sugar cookie dough with more force than strictly necessary. "It's unhygienic to have all those chickens running around loose. And where else are we going to store hay?"

"I just don't know, dear." Mabel paused in her drawer-rummage. "Papa always looked after the barn, and without him here, it just seems like too big an undertaking."

"Don't be ridiculous." A little sprinkle of flour kept the rolling pin from sticking. I reached for the cookie cutter and stamped out six rabbits before I realized what I was holding: the coveted bunny cookie cutter.

"Where did you find this?" I certainly wasn't going to cry over a scrap of metal, but I came close.

"It was in the drawer, right where it always is." She looked me over, perhaps seeing for a second that I wasn't the Elizabeth they thought I was. Close, in my green calico apron and braided coronet of hair and dimpled mouth, but not identical.

"We can speak to Mama about it. But I know what she'll say."

"Out of the question," Addie broke in. "That's what she'll say."

"Why?" I wiped the flour off my hands so I could put them on my hips. I hoped I looked defiant. Meemaw always said Addie Mae admired spunk in her girls.

"You mind your manners, or I'll slap you out the back-door," she said.

So much for spunk.

"Just where are you keeping all the cows in the meantime, eh? Next thing we know, someone will step in a big stinking pile of cowsh—"

"Language, please!" Addie Mae did her best not to laugh, but nothing could hide the glimmer of a smile that twitched at her lips. "Remember you are a lady and not a farmhand."

"She has a point, Mama." Mabel paused, wooden spoon in hand. "We need a place to put the pigs—"

Addie Mae and I exclaimed in one horrified voice: "Pigs?!"

"And Elizabeth could use the hayloft as a studio, seeing as how her old one disappeared."

Addie Mae considered my clasped hands, pleading face and my very best attempt at puppy-dog eyes. Then she drew me close for a floury kiss on the cheek.

"All right then. But don't come running to me when the mice get in the hay."

"That's what cats are for!" I galloped out the back door with a whoop of triumph, apron strings flapping. The barn, Elizabeth's hidey-hole studio . . . my art had to be there. I ran down the flagstone path and paused at the garden gate to holler my thanks over my shoulder—

But the scene that lay before me stole the words from my mouth. The house was just as I remembered it, every brick, every green tendril of ivy. Trees stood in a protective sentinel circle around her, relenting only for the driveway lined with berry vines. Behind a thin curtain of mist, I could just make out the beginnings of the orchard and my barn.

I had to call Meemaw and tell her what's happened. But

would she believe me? There were times, sitting in the kitchen with the Great Aunts gathered around me, that I scarcely believed myself. And if she believed, what would she say when she discovered there was only room here for one Elizabeth, and that was me.

I clung to the fencepost for a moment. I couldn't think about that now, Scarlett. I had paintings to find and a show to put on.

The barn was just where it should have been. Once upon a different time, it was a gray weathered tangle of planks and yellow-green moss. I ran my hand over rough new wood still sticky with resin then pulled the door open. Hay bales were stacked in a prickly blockade and the requisite marmalade cat dozed in a patch of mellow sunshine.

I scrambled up the ladder to the hayloft, nearly falling in my haste and getting a palm full of splinters. I blinked the tears from my eyes and poked my head through the hatch, greeted not by the welcome sight of my purloined artwork but by a sad-faced Elizabeth.

"They're not here."

"Are you sure?" The letdown wasn't unexpected, but still unwelcome. I prowled around, poked through the bits of straw. There was no place for them to hide, really. I flopped down in defeat. "Well, shit."

Elizabeth knelt next to me and put her thin hand on my shoulder. "I'm terribly sorry. Maybe you could make new pieces for the show?"

"In a day?" I rested my forehead against my knees. "That was months' worth of work."

Elizabeth sighed. "It's a pity all this domesticity isn't very artistic. There's certainly plenty of it hanging around."

The flower-strewn pattern of her apron caught my eye. I pleated it with half my attention. The hamster in my brain took the other half and ran with it.

"Maybe you're right." Inspiration tingled, like sticking my finger in an electrical outlet.

Elizabeth started; she must have felt it too. "I am?"

"You are. Didn't Mabel say something about the trunks in the attic?" I felt a mad glimmer dance its way through me. My fingers twitched for some vintage lace, satin ribbons and my glue gun.

I grabbed her hand. "Come on. We need to get back to the house. I'll need everyone's help."

Elizabeth held back, pulled her hand from mine.

"There's only room for one Elizabeth—"

"And that's *you*," I said, and stuck out my hand. "I'm Lizbit, and the pleasure is mine."

"It looks just lovely," Mabel twittered from the depths of my purse. "I especially like the pyramid of jam."

That particular installation stood over ten feet tall and glittered with the glass-trapped jewel tones of summers past. Two-part invisible epoxy held the jars in place, and I'd already heard murmurs about toast and crépes from more than one patron.

It wasn't the only success. Hours of careful stitching and a lot of starch got five quilts folded into origami cranes; Double Wedding Ring, Egg Money and Ring Around the Nine-Patch sported "Sold" stickers. Mabel had devoted herself to "The March of the Rabbit Army," rolling, cutting, baking and frosting until the wee hours. Already two people had gotten stern lectures from security for attempting to eat the art.

"I think we can safely say that our girl is a hit," Addie Mae added, her voice muffled by a wad of Kleenex and a lipstick; I really should clean out my purse. "And you did an excellent job with the fried chicken."

I had to agree; it was amusing to see critics gnawing on chicken legs wrapped in checkered napkins. The one who skewered my previous show waved to me with half a biscuit.

"Marvelous, darling. Simply too fabulous for words."

My agent hugged me hard and towed me off to the side to hiss in my ear.

"I got an offer on the pen-and-ink sketch."

I shook my head. "It's not for sale."

"Everything is for sale, darling. He says to name your price." She jerked her thumb at a man wearing linen pants, suitably rumpled.

"It's not for sale," I repeated. "Have you tried the pie?"

Scoops of ice cream replaced the dollar signs in her eyes. "What kind?"

"Apple slice, just how you like." I grinned as she scurried off. Then I sneaked another look at Mr. Big Offer.

"He's charming," said Elva.

"I wonder who his people are," said Olive.

"He's a purebred. I'd bet my coral necklace on it," said Elizabeth.

"But he wants Lizbit's pen-and-ink—"

My eyes traveled to the picture; one that I'd pulled out of my portfolio at five this morning, shaking with exhaustion and adrenaline. I'd drawn it years ago. I knew every brick, every tendril of ivy. And it wasn't for sale. Not to anyone. Not at any price.

"What's it called?" His voice, like coffee with cream, wasn't entirely unexpected.

I turned to him with my grandmother's smile.

"Homecoming." I got a better grip on my purse, mindful of the brick inside, and accepted his proffered elbow.

Ekaterina Sedia's first novel, According to Crow, *was published by Five Star Books. Her second,* The Secret History of Moscow, *is coming in early 2008 from Prime Books. Her short stories sold to* Analog, Baen's Universe, Fantasy Magazine, *and* Dark Wisdom, *and* Japanese Dreams *and* Magic in the Mirrorstone *anthologies. Visit her website at* www.ekaterinasedia.com

ZOMBIE LENIN

Ekaterina Sedia

1.

It all started when I was eight years old, on a school trip to the Mausoleum. My mom was there to chaperon my class, and it was nice, because she held me when I got nauseous on the bus. I remember the cotton tights all the girls wore, and how they bunched on our knees and slid down, so that we had to hike them up, as discreetly as eight-year-olds could. It was October, and my coat was too short; mom said it was fine even though its belt came disconcertingly close to my underarms, and the coat didn't even cover my butt. I didn't believe her; I frowned at the photographer as he aligned his camera, pinning my mom and me against the backdrop of the St. Basil's Cathedral. "Smile," mom whispered. We watched the change of guard in front of the Mausoleum.

Then we went inside. At that time, I was still vague on what it was that we were supposed to see. I followed in small mincing steps down the grim marble staircase along with the line of people as they descended and filed into a large hall and looked to their right. I looked too, to see a small yellowing man in a dark suit under a glass bell. His eyes were closed, and he was undeniably dead. The air of an inanimate object hung dense, like the smell of artificial flowers. When I shuffled past him, looking, looking, unable to turn away, his eyes snapped open and he sat up in a jerking motion of a marionette, shattering the glass bubble around him. I screamed.

2.

"A dead woman is the ultimate sex symbol," someone behind me says.

His interlocutor laughs. "Right. To a necrophile maybe."

"No, no," the first man says, heatedly. "Think of every old novel you've ever read. The heroine who's too sexually liberated for her time usually dies. Ergo, a dead woman is dead because she was too sexually transgressive."

"This is just dumb, Fedya," says the second man. "What, Anna Karenina is a sex symbol?"

"Of course. That one's trivial. But also every other woman who ever died."

I stare at the surface of the plastic cafeteria table. It's cheap and pockmarked with burns, their edges rough under my fingers. I drink my coffee and listen intently for the two men behind me to speak again.

"Undine," the first one says. "Rusalki. All of them dead, all of them irresistible to men."

I finish my coffee and stand up. I glance at the guy who spoke—he's young, my age, with light clear eyes of a madman.

"Euridice," I whisper as I pass.

3.

The lecturer is old, his beard dirty-yellow with age, his trembling fingers stained with nicotine. I sit all the way in the back, my eyes closed, listening, and occasionally drifting off to dream-sleep.

"Chthonic deities," he says. "The motif of resurrection. Who can tell me what is the relationship between the two?"

We remain wisely silent.

"The obstacle," he says. "The obstacle to resurrection. Ereshkigal, Hades, Hel. All of them hold the hero hostage and demand a ransom of some sort."

His voice drones on, talking about the price one pays, and about Persephone being an exception as she's not quite dead. But Euridice, oh she gets it big time. I wonder if Persephone or Euridice is a better sex symbol and if one should compare the two.

"Zombies," the voice says, "are in violation. Their resurrection bears no price and has no meaning. The soul and the body separated are a terrible thing. It is punitive, not curative." His yellow beard trembles, bald patch on his skull shines in a slick of parchment skin, one of his eyes fake and popping. He sits up and reaches for me.

I scream and jerk awake.

"Bad dream?" the lecturer says, without any particular mockery or displeasure. "It happens. When you dream your soul travels to the Underworld."

"Chthonic deities," I mumble. "I'm sorry."

"That's right," he says. "Chthonic."

4.

When I was eight, I had nightmares about that visit. I dreamt of the dead yellowing man chasing me up and down the stairs of our apartment building. I still have those dreams. I'm running past the squeezing couples and smokers exiled to the stairwell, and mincing steps are chasing after me. I skip over the steps, jumping over two at once, three at once, throwing myself into each stairwell as if it were a pool. Soon my feet are barely touching the steps as I rush downward in an endless spiral of chipped stairs. I'm flying in fear as the dead man is following. He's much slower than me but he does not stop, so I cannot stop either.

"Zombies," he calls after me into the echoey stairwell, "are the breach of covenant. If the chthonic deities do not get their blood-price, there can be no true resurrection."

I wake up with a start. My stomach hurts.

5.

I take the subway to the university. I usually read so I don't have to meet people's eyes. "Station Lenin Hills," the announcer on the intercom says. "The doors are closing. Next station is the University."

I look up and see the guy who spoke of dead women sitting across from me. His eyes, bleached with insanity, stare at me with the black pinpricks of the pupils. He pointedly ignores the old woman in a black kerchief standing too close to him, trying to guilt him into surrendering his seat. He doesn't get up until I do, when the train pulls into the station. "The University," the announcer says.

We exit together.

"I'm Fedya," he says.

"I'm afraid of zombies," I answer.

He doesn't look away.

6.

The lecturer's eyes water with age. He speaks directly to me when he asks, "Any other resurrection myths you know of?"

"Jesus?" someone from the first row says.

He nods. "And what was the price paid for his resurrection?"

"There wasn't one," I say, startling myself. "He was a zombie."

This time everyone stares.

"Talk to me after class," the lecturer says.

7.

The chase across all the stairwells in the world becomes a game. He catches up to me now. I'm too tired to be afraid enough to wake up. My stomach hurts.

"You cannot break the covenant with chthonic gods," he tells me. "Some resurrection is the punishment."

"Leave me alone," I plead. "What have I ever done to you?"

His fake eye, icy-blue, steely-grey, slides down his ruined cheek. "You can't save them," he says. "They always look back. They always stay dead."

"Like with Euridice."

"Like with every dead woman."

8.

Fedya sits on my bed, heavily although he's not a large man but slender, birdlike.

"I could never drive a car," I tell him.

He looks at the yellowing medical chart, dog-eared pages fanned on the bed covers. "Sluggish schizophrenia?" he says. "This is a bullshit diagnosis. You know it as well as I do. Delusions of reformism? You know that they invented it as a punitive thing."

"It's not bullshit," I murmur. It's not. Injections of sulfazine and the rubber room had to have a reason behind them.

"They kept you in the Serbsky hospital," he observes. "Serbsky? I didn't know you were a dissident."

"Lenin is a zombie," I tell him. "He talks to me." All these years. All this medication.

He stares. "I can't believe they let you into the university."

I shrug. "They don't pay attention to that anymore."

"Maybe things are changing," he says.

9.

"Are you feeling all right?" the lecturer says, his yellow hands shaking, filling me with quiet dread. Same beard, same bald patch.

I nod.

"Where did that zombie thing come from?" he asks, concerned.

"You said it yourself. Chthonic deities always ask for a price. If you don't pay, you stay dead or become a zombie. Women stay dead."

He lifts his eyebrows encouragingly. "Oh?"

"Dead are objects," I tell him. "Don't you know that? Some would rather become zombies than objects. Only zombies are still objects, even though they don't think they are."

I can see that he wants to laugh but decides not to. "And why do you think women decide to stay dead?"

I feel nauseous and think of Inanna who kind of ruins my thesis. I ignore her. "It has something to do with sex," I say miserably.

He really tries not to laugh.

10.

In the hospital, when I lay in a sulfazine-and-neuroleptics coma, he would sit on the edge of my bed. "You know what they say about me."

"Yes," I whispered, my cheeks so swollen that they squeezed my eyes shut. "Lenin is more alive than any of the living."

"And what is life?"

"According to Engels, it's a mode of existence of protein bodies."

"I am a protein body," he said. "What do you have to say to that?"

"I want to go home," I whispered with swollen lips. "Why can't you leave me alone?"

He didn't answer, but his waxen fingers stroked my cheek, leaving a warm melting trail behind them.

11.

"I thought for sure you were a cutter," Fedya says.

I shiver in my underwear and hug my shoulders. My skin

puckers in the cold breeze from the window. "I'm not." I feel compelled to add, "Sorry."

"You can get dressed now," he says.

I do.

He watches.

12.

The professor is done with chthonic deities, and I lose interest. I drift through the dark hallways, where the walls are so thick that they still retain the cold of some winter from many years ago. I poke my head into one auditorium, and listen a bit to a small sparrow of a woman chatter about Kant. I stop by the stairwell on the second floor, to bum a cigarette off a fellow student with black horn-rimmed glasses.

"Skipping class?" she says.

"Just looking for something to do."

"You can come to my class," she says. "It's pretty interesting."

"What is it about?"

"Economics."

I finish my smoke and tag along.

This lecturer looks like mine, and I take for a sign. I sit in an empty seat in the back, and listen. "The idea of capitalism rests on the concept of free market," he says. "Who can tell me what it is?"

No one can, or wants to.

The lecturer notices me. "What do you think? Yes, you, the young lady who thinks it's a good idea to waltz in in the middle of the class. What is free market?"

"It's when you pay the right price," I say. "To the chthonic deities. If you don't pay you become a zombie or just stay dead."

He stares at me. "I don't think you're in the right class."

13.

I sit in the stairwell of the second floor. Lenin emerges from the brass stationary ashtray and sits next to me. There's one floor up and one down, and nowhere really to run.

"What have you learned today?" he asks in an almost paternal voice.

"Free market," I tell him.

He shakes his head. "It will end the existence of the protein bodies in a certain mode." A part of his cheek is peeling off.

"Remember when I was in the hospital?"

"Of course. Those needles hurt. You cried a lot."

I nod. "My boyfriend doesn't like me."

"I'm sorry," he says. "If it makes it any better, I will leave soon."

I realize that I would miss him. He followed me since I was little. "Is it because of the free market?" I ask. "I'm sorry. I'll go back to the chthonic deities."

"It's not easy," he says and stands up, his joints whirring, his skin shedding like sheets of wax paper. He walks away on soft rubbery legs.

14.

"Things die eventually," I tell Fedya. "Even those that are not quite dead to begin with."

"Yeah, and?" he answers and drinks his coffee.

I stroke the melted circles in the plastic, like craters on

the lunar surface. "One doesn't have to be special to die. One has to be special to stay dead. This is why you like Euridice, don't you?"

He frowns. "Is that the one Orpheus followed to Hades?"

"Yes. Only he followed her the wrong way."

15.

There is a commotion on the second floor, and the stairwell is isolated from the corridor by a black sheet. The ambulances are howling outside, and distraught smokers crowd the hallway, cut off from their usual smoking place.

I ask a student from my class what's going on. He tells me that the chthonic lecturer has collapsed during the lecture about the hero's journey. "Heart attack, probably."

I push my way through the crowd, just in time to see the paramedics carry him off. I see the stooped back of a balding dead man following the paramedics and their burden, not looking back. Some students cry.

"He just died during the lecture," a girl's voice behind me says. "He just hit the floor and died."

I watch the familiar figure on uncertain soft legs walk downstairs in a slow mincing shuffle, looking to his right at the waxen profile with an upturned beard staring into the sky from the gurney. The lecturer and zombie Lenin disappear from my sight, and I turn away. "Stay dead," I whisper. "Don't look back."

The rest is up to them and chthonic deities.

Jeremiah Tolbert is a hairless bipedal ape spotted by unreliable witnesses in the foothills of Colorado, but experts claim that his species is native to Kansas. Rumor has it that he shadowed two sasquatch hunting expeditions hoping to get a story from the experience. When he sat down to write one, he wrote this instead.

THE YETI BEHIND YOU

Jeremiah Tolbert

Michael's yeti sits lightly on the foot of the bed, watching with soft brown eyes as Michael makes a third pass at tying his tie. He mumbles "Around the tree, under the log," but he's speaking only to himself, not to his silent observer. He is careful not to speak to it.

Michael first noticed the yeti when he awoke sometime during the night, his bladder full of passed beer. Blinking in the dim red light of alarm clock numerals, he'd stared at a hulking figure leaning against the closet doorframe. All he could make out was the humanoid shape. Confident that the beast was a delusion of sleep, he climbed from the bed quietly, shuffled past, careful not to acknowledge or come into contact with it, and went to the bathroom. When he returned, he was surprised—but somehow not disturbed—to see that the yeti remained. Despite its presence, he slept until the alarm screeched hours later.

Michael looks over the yeti before leaving the bedroom. He thinks of it as a yeti because its fur is white. If the fur was brown, he would think of it as a sasquatch or a bigfoot. Probably sasquatch, because it sounds less demeaning. He once half-watched a special on the Discovery Channel about people who hunted such things. Half-watched because he was also trying to read *Pregnancy Today* at Beth's insistence; he would have rather watched the special, even though he thought the idea of such a large undiscovered animal ridiculous. The Himalayas, on the other hand . . . who knows? Asia is big.

Michael leaves the bedroom and the yeti stands and follows. It has to crouch and turn sideways to squeeze through the door. In the living room, with its high, vaulted ceiling, the yeti straightens up to its full and impressive height, and stretches its thick arms up above its head. Michael hopes that it won't try to fit into his car.

As Michael climbs clumsily out of his Saturn, a red Ford pickup pulls into the space next to his. A shaggy, reddish mammoth trundles behind it. The mammoth comes to a halt inches from the Ford's bumper and lifts its trunk high in the air, swaying it side to side. The yeti watches the mammoth closely for a moment, then returns its gaze to Michael, blinking.

The owner of the Ford pickup is a loan officer from the front office. "Morning," she says, stepping out of her truck.

He hopes that the loan officer will see his yeti, but she does not, nor does she give any indication that she is aware of the mammoth following her. Hibbets holds the door open for her, and irritably motions for Michael to hurry. Hibbets is not a man to be kept waiting. Michael nearly steps on the small herd of trilobites clustered at Hibbets' feet. They shuffle around the CEO on dainty, chitinous legs, their bodies the size of small dinner plates.

Michael's yeti waits for him in the lobby.

Michael takes frequent coffee breaks, even though the caffeine makes him jittery and he finds the taste too bitter. He doesn't recognize many of the animals, but Google knows all, and identifying the animals is time consuming but not terribly difficult. At lunch, the employee parking lot is full of sauropods and Pleistocene mammals that are too large to squeeze inside the building. A Triceratops, his favorite dinosaur when he was a boy, mingles with a giant sloth and something resembling a nine foot tall carnivorous duck with a bill shaped like an axe. Moas, looking like shaggy-dog ostriches, roam the halls of the office. Marsupial lions and miniature horses guard the entrances to cubicles.

The observers are all members of an extinct species. At first, Michael thought that his own yeti might be an exception—being that a yeti is a mythological creature, not an extinct one—but then he discovered *Gigantopithecus blacki* on a primatologist's website. The males weighed twelve hundred pounds and stood ten feet tall, but the females were smaller. Michael believes that his silent observer is a female. He considers the name of *Gigantopithecus*, but ultimately discards it. Yeti is easier to remember.

He finds an interesting quote that he prints out, nervously pacing around the laser printer as it warms up and finally prints. Hibbets would pitch a fit if he found anyone using the printers for personal reasons.

Michael snatches up the printout and reads it once aloud.

"An old Sherpa once observed: 'There is a yeti in the back of everyone's mind; only the blessed are not haunted by it.'" He stares at the paper for a few moments after speaking the words aloud, then crumples the sheet into a ball and stuffs it into his pocket before returning to his desk.

He calls home, but Beth doesn't answer. She sleeps all day, now. He leaves work early. It's hell getting out of the parking lot without running over anything.

He drives to the mountains. He turns off the radio and hums tunelessly as the terrain outside grows steeper.

Snow is thick on the ground, the pine trees frosted like conical birthday cakes. The road ends short of the peak, a wall seven feet high of impenetrable snow rising up from the blacktop just beyond the barrier. Along the pull-off, snow-mobilers load their trailers, all red-faced and exhausted. A crocodile-thing on long, dog-like legs watches from a snow bank, oblivious to the cold. Overhead, a pterodactyl circles lazily on invisible and impossible thermal currents.

He steps outside the car into the biting air and the yeti appears from behind a tree. He walks onto the hard packed snow beneath the anorexic alpine forest. The yeti follows. She leaves no tracks.

He walks into an open space, stands in the middle, and turns to face the yeti. She stops and returns his stare. The wind dies. Snow settles against more snow, pressing against the cold, hard soil. The yeti parts her lips, as if about to speak. Michael inhales sharply. The yeti catches a snowflake on the pink-gray tip of her tongue. He exhales, and turns and heads back to the car. It would have been too easy.

The yeti crouches in the muddy strip of weed and grass between the sidewalk and the curb in front of Michael's house. She picks at the dirt with a stick, looking up only when he closes the car door. Michael can see his wife inside through the screen door, reading on the couch, book perched gently atop the mound of her growing belly. The yeti turns to stare too.

He sits for a long time, until the sun sets. The yeti follows him in. Beth pays her no attention. She looks up and smiles. "How was work? I didn't know you were going to be late." For once, her tone isn't accusatory.

"Same old thing, just more of it," he mumbles, moving toward the bathroom. It is too small for the yeti to fit inside. He closes the door, puts the toilet seat down, and sits on top of it. Outside, Beth asks, "Where's my kiss?" in a hurt tone.

"Just a minute," he says. He flips through a magazine, but he thinks about the yeti out there, all alone with his wife and the baby. He flushes, and doesn't bother pretending to wash his hands, opens the door, and forces a smile.

Beth eases off the couch and wraps her arms around his neck, pulling him into a kiss. He closes his eyes. He feels the yeti standing just over his shoulder, her arms hanging limp at her sides. He pulls away from Beth reluctantly. "I'm hungry," he says, even though he isn't. "What do you want tonight?"

Beth frowns. "I was craving walnuts earlier. Isn't that weird? Now I'm just hungry. Whatever you want." She pats her belly and grins.

Michael pretends to think. Given a choice, he'd eat the same thing every day. "Let's order pizza. Watch a movie." He pulls Beth onto the couch beside him, careful of her belly. He calls and orders a large pie with pepperoni on one half and artichoke hearts on the other. The yeti slips past them and sits in his La-Z-Boy.

Michael lets Beth pick the movie. They watch an old Jim Henson film called *Labyrinth*. It's her favorite movie, but Michael finds it off; David Bowie's look hasn't aged well with time. The yeti leans forward in the chair whenever Ludo—a tall, red-furred ape-like monster—is on screen. Her fingers dance, and she hesitantly reaches for the screen, then jerks her hand back when the fingertips graze the glass. Michael is suddenly flooded with sorrow.

After Beth falls asleep—just before the final battle in the Goblin City—Michael steps onto the porch to watch the evening strollers and the animals that silently follow. The yeti joins him. It's like history parading past. Michael thinks about asking her a question, but to address her would be to acknowledge the beast as reality. To acknowledge that would be to acknowledge something much worse about himself.

He stands there watching, and sometime later Beth wakes and stands beside him in the doorway.

"You're thinking about the baby again," she says.

He's not, but he can't say why. He nods instead.

"I'm sorry," she whispers.

"It's not your fault," he says. "It's a baby. It's nobody's fault. Or we're both at fault."

"Are you afraid?" she asks. The yeti turns her head toward Michael.

He doesn't answer for a moment. "Yes. Of course," he says. "Aren't you?"

Her brow furrows. "I worry . . . "

"I dreamed about this once," he says. "It's a little person. It's not like a . . . a dog. If it doesn't work out, you're stuck with it. Responsible until it grows old enough to take care of itself."

She smiles. "And sometimes, even longer."

The panic grips him again; he sweats, his heart races, his hands go numb. "I feel trapped." He looks away. The door slams shut.

The yeti watches without a sound.

"Why are you here?" he demands.

Almost imperceptibly, the yeti shrugs.

Saturday morning, and the yeti watches cartoons. Michael always turns on the TV in the morning while he does the little chores and tasks that have piled up through the week. Lately, the yeti has been paying less attention to him. She watches Beth whenever she is in the room, but this morning, she still sleeps. The baby's kicks kept her awake the night before.

"I don't suppose you could help me fold the laundry," he asks the yeti. She doesn't answer. "I didn't think so."

The bedroom door opens, and Beth's sleepy head pokes out. "Who are you talking to?"

"Just the TV," he says.

"Weirdo," she says.

"That's me."

"Would you do me a favor, my love?"

"Can't," he says, giving her a theatrical helpless shrug. "Folding laundry."

She mock scowls. "I need walnuts."

He snatches up his keys from the corner table, grinning.

"I love you!" she calls out as he passes through the door.

"I love you, too," he says back. "I don't mean you," he whispers to the yeti. She stands between them, looking back at Beth.

Michael steps around someone's dodo and examines cans of nuts. The store has pecans, peanuts, and various mixed nuts, but no canned walnuts. He wanders the isles, avoiding the help and their observers. After a while, he notices the yeti is gone.

He finds her in the baking supplies, next to bags of chopped walnuts. She points to them, and then folds her arms across her chest. He wonders what her posture means in yeti. She looks almost self-satisfied. He sticks his tongue out at her. A woman, surrounded by hairless rats the size of poodles, scowls at him from behind the yeti. Michael pays in the express checkout lane. A Tasmanian tiger sits at the end of the counter, keeping one eye on the clerk. It looks vaguely bored.

"I'm sorry," he says, placing the walnuts on the table. Beth doesn't look up from her book.

"They didn't have any?"

"No. For what I said."

"Oh." She turns the page.

"I can't help how I feel," he says.

"Is that so?"

"I'm still here," he says.

"That you are," she answers, looking up. "And that's something."

———

Later, he goes for a drive. He takes the Cherokee. The yeti rides in the passenger seat, slumped low with her knees tucked up below her breasts.

"How long you've been here?" he says. "I wonder if you met my father."

As usual, she says nothing.

"If Beth had met him, she would understand."

The yeti hoots softly. Michael is so startled, he nearly hits a tree. He pulls over and calms himself before driving home, pushing a little over the speed limit until reaching his street.

Michael pulls up next to the house. Beth is sitting on the steps of the porch, clutching her stomach. Her face is a mask of agony. Michael feels panic rising. He opens the door, freezes. Something shoves him hard, and he stumbles onto the street. It is just the momentum he needs. He kicks open the gate and rushes to Beth's side. "What happened?" he shouts.

"Hospital," she says weakly.

He breaks the speed limit by twenty the whole way. The yeti rides in the back seat. She rocks from side to side, her arms around her bony knees.

"Just a bad case of indigestion, I'm sure," the doctor says, and a strange blue crab scuttles behind him as he paces the ER room. Beth lays on the bed, and by the look on her face, she wants to grab him and shout at him to plant his feet. It took her two years to beat the habit out of Michael. It's taken something like this to bring it back.

Michael sits in a chair next to her. The yeti squeezes into the corner behind him. Her head grazes the sound paneling above. For a crazy moment while the admitter checked them in, he wondered if he should ask if yetis were unsanitary. He wasn't sure if the yeti would listen to him if he asked her to stay outside though.

Now, he thinks hard about his breathing. He is thinking, *slow, slow, slow.*

When the doctor leaves, Beth lets herself cry, a mixture of anger and relief. "How could I be so silly?" she asks. Michael doesn't answer. He repeats his mantra.

Beth waves her hand at him. "Hello, Michael?"

He blinks. "I couldn't move," he says. "When I saw you, I couldn't move."

"But you did," she says. "You helped me into the car."

"She shoved me," he says.

Beth squints. "Who did?"

"My yeti."

"Your what?"

"My imaginary extinct animal." The yeti heads for the door.

"I see."

"I'm sorry."

"Just leave, Michael."

For once, he follows the yeti, instead of the other way around.

His yeti stands in front of the car. He turns the key, and the engine starts up. The yeti doesn't move.

"Get in," he says.

The yeti slowly cups her arms, and rocks them back and forth. Her soft brown eyes bore into Michael. He turns off the ignition.

"What?" he asks. "Yeah, the baby. The baby's fine. Beth's fine. Everybody's fine."

She shakes her head.

Michael's resolve cracks and before he knows it, he's sobbing. He rushes back inside the hospital, past the admitter, past security, ignoring their protests. He finds the doctor two doors down. "Check again," he shouts. "Check her again."

Security guards have Michael by the arms. He sits in a seat in the lobby. One mutters something about the police being on their way. The emergency doors swing open wide and the doctor steps into the lobby. He motions to the guards, and they reluctantly release Michael.

"I don't know how," the doctor says, shaking his head. "She's going to be fine. Now. I'm sorry we didn't catch the problem earlier, it . . . "

"What about my baby?"

No answer.

"What about my *baby*, you son of a bitch?"

Outside, something howls to the rising new moon, and Michael's panic rises to meet it.

"It's too soon to say," says the doctor.

Michael wheels Beth out of the hospital and into the warm spring air. She gasps, and points to the car. "What is that?"

The yeti stands beside the passenger door, watching them. Michael's not surprised that Beth can see her. He doesn't have the energy for it.

"*Gigantapithecus blacki*," he says. "But yeti is easier to remember."

"That's your imaginary extinct animal?" she asks.

"I think she's *our* imaginary extinct animal," he says. "Are you scared?"

"Of her? No. I don't know why. Or do you mean about us?"

He shrugs. He means both.

"You didn't have to come back," she says, as he helps her from the chair into the jeep. "But you did."

"I wouldn't have left," he says. "I'm afraid, but I'm not a coward." But he isn't sure that is the truth; he thinks maybe that's just what he wants to believe.

"We're having a baby, Michael," she says suddenly. "Oh my God, we're having a baby."

Michael turns the ignition, and backs out. "We sure are, my love."

Behind them, the yeti chuckles so quietly the noise could be only tires on pavement. There is a hint of sadness of it. Michael remembers asking why she was here, and her shrug to deflect the question. Somehow, he thinks, she didn't want to share the sadness with which she and the other lost ones are burdened. They're all here for the same reason; all watching for the moments they will never have again.

He reaches across and squeezes Beth's hand slowly, slowly, slowly.

Amanda Downum lives in Texas with her husband and cats, and works in a university library to support her growing brood of baby novels. Her short fiction is published in Realms of Fantasy *and* Strange Horizons. *For more information about her and her work, visit* www.amandadownum.com *This story was inspired by a few B horror movies, and a fascination with catacombs and terrible angels.*

THE SALVATION GAME

Amanda Downum

The labyrinth swallows light and leaves no bones. Darkness laughs at Lily's flashlight, low chuckles echoing from every footstep. She trails her left hand along the cold stone wall, groping for an opening.

Keep turning left, the witch said.

Her breath sounds too harsh and loud to be her own, some snuffling minotaur stalking her through the dark. The birthmark below her left breast tingles in time with her heartbeat.

Danny is still alive, and close.

Her fingers find a corner and she turns, flashlight beam sliding off more stone, more shadows. Grit crunches under her boots; silt coats her hand, itches on her face. The air is too heavy, full of dust that sifted down from rocks cut centuries before she was born. Full of time.

She's deep below now, the weight of earth and stone pressing close around her, the weight of the cathedral soaring far over her head. Worlds away, those spires and arches, echoing vaults and jeweled Mucha glass. Even farther the city, the hum of traffic and voices, lights and music, everything real.

Adrenaline stings her cheeks, roils queasy in her stomach, and the urge to turn and run is so strong she shakes. But her brother is alive at the center of the maze. She'll find him. She'll bring him out. She has to.

"Are you frightened?" The woman called Gethsemane lounged against velvet cushions, watching Lily through dancing shadows. Candles burned in bowls of colored glass, fitful flicker like trapped fireflies.

"Yes." Lily's voice was dry and fragile as mothwings.

"But you came anyway."

"I don't know where else to go." Lily tried to meet the woman's gaze, but caught only flashes of white skin and black ink. Six months of searching and questioning, six months of dead ends, of people who wouldn't talk to her or had nothing to say. Six months and she ended up here, in this dark room that smelled of poppy spice and anise, of something musky and autumnal. Like snakes. She could only pray that this wasn't another dead-end, another waste of time.

"There is nowhere else. Not if you mean to act quickly." Gethsemane leaned forward. Tattoos swirled across the curve of her shaven head, spilled out of her sleeves onto her hands. Shadows limned razor cheekbones, turned her eyes into black pools. Lily's skin crawled, cold sweat prickling her scalp, but the tingle over her heart held her when she wanted to flee.

"Can you help me?"

"You were clever to get this far, to find me. You've taken

risks, put yourself in danger."

She was so tired of playing games. "I need to help my brother. Can you help me?"

"Need is a dangerous thing. I can help you, but what will you do for me?"

Lily swallowed. "Whatever it takes."

"That's a bold promise, and a foolish one. Is your brother really worth so much to you?"

"He's my brother."

The woman cocked a dark eyebrow. "That doesn't entirely answer the question, my dear."

"I have to help him. If I'd—" She stopped, shook her head.

"Go on," Gethsemane said, raising one long white hand. "If . . . ?"

"If I'd found him earlier, this wouldn't have happened. I should never have let him run off."

"Ahh. So this is about you, then. Your guilt."

Lily's jaw tightened and her cheeks warmed. "My brother is in danger. I need to find him. If you won't help me—"

Gethsemane chuckled. "If I won't help you, then you're quite fucked, aren't you?"

Lily's fingernails bit her palms. "Please."

The postcards started a year after Danny ran away. Montreal, London, Vienna, Prague, pictures of cathedrals, of subways, of twisting cobbled alleys, notes written in childhood sibling code. She didn't know how he managed to travel, what he did for money, but the cards said he was all right, and she believed him, because she would have known if he wasn't.

She dreamed of him, too. Lost dreams, happy dreams, sad

and wanting dreams. Dreams of strangers and strange places. Eventually she learned to put them aside, shove them down so they didn't haunt her during the day. He said he was happy, and she told herself that was all that mattered.

She was happy in the home he'd fled, happy with the family who'd taken her in, the first safe and stable home she'd known in years. And she was happy—alone in the dark where she could whisper the truth to herself—to have someone looking after her for a change, instead of her constant desperation to keep Danny safe, to keep their mother out of trouble. She'd failed in that, but it had set her free. For five years she dealt with that distant echo in the back of her mind. For five years she built a life for herself—family, friends, school, all the simple things she thought she'd never have.

Then the cards stopped, and the nightmares started. Dreams of angels and altars, of dark winged things, with eyes all full of emptiness and stars.

Then her birthmark, their twin-mark, that bruise-blue shadow over both their hearts, began to sting and throb. And Lily knew her brother needed her again.

She followed Gethsemane's directions to Prague, into Old Town, through bitter November rain. Icy water soaked her collar, chased away the jetlag dragging at her eyes. Somewhere nearby the Orloj chimed the hour.

As Lily neared the Chorea, she knew the witch hadn't lied. Her head echoed with the overlap of someone else's thoughts. After so many years it dizzied her, and she paused on the narrow cobbled street as the night spun around her in a blur of light and stinging rain. She heard music, felt the ghost-touch of hands on someone else's skin. She felt Danny tense, knew he felt her too.

The miasma of the club enveloped her as she descended the narrow cellar stair, sound and smoke and sweat, crawling into her ears and mouth and burning her eyes. Beneath the reek of cigarettes and bodies the air was thick with incense, patchouli and wine and rot-sweet roses. She worked her dry tongue against the roof of her mouth, swallowed the taste of old pennies. The dance floor sucked her in and she moved with the current, swirled through the tangle of bodies and let it spit her out on the other side.

She found him lounging in a wide booth against the far wall. Half a stranger now—baby-fat melted away, his hair bleached platinum-pale and shorter than he used to wear it—but she knew him. Two girls draped themselves around him; with their wild black hair and matching leopard-skin dresses they looked more like twins than Lily and Danny. All three stared at her with glassy dark eyes as she approached.

Danny blinked. "I thought I was imagining it. I didn't think you'd really come." His voice was slurred, and he'd picked up a hint of accent.

Seven years like a river between them, dark and wide. Then Danny stood, shook off the clinging girls and stumbled into Lily's arms.

"What are you doing here?"

"I'm here for you." She caught his arms, looked up at his face—farther than she'd had to look up before. She leaned in, enunciating over the throb of the music. "Something's going to happen."

He smiled a stranger's smile, wry and amused and so much

older than the boy she remembered. "Always looking out for me. Always so serious."

Lily started to reply, then paused. His shirt hung open, revealing a dark mark on his chest. She pushed aside sweat-damp fabric; a tattoo covered his heart, black and yellow ink swirling in queasy streaks, a twisting three-armed spiral eclipsing the birthmark.

"What's this?" She touched the design, scrubbed her fingertips on her pants.

He caught her hand. "It's—a long story. Seven years long. I've learned things, seen things."

Lily frowned. "You sound like Mom."

"It's all real, Lily, everything she used to talk about. Angels and stars and doors. I've seen all of it."

"Mom was crazy." Which didn't make the monsters any less real. Lily had seen enough already to know that.

"She was. She didn't understand—she couldn't deal with it. But I've seen the truth. You wouldn't believe—"

A hand fell on Danny's shoulder and the resonance between them dissolved. A dark-haired man leaned close to his ear. "Čas vypršel, Daniel. We should go."

Danny blinked, strobe lights shining in his glassy eyes. "Yeah, of course. Just a sec."

The man glanced at Lily, eyes narrow, then nodded and stepped back. The leopard girls crawled out of the booth and fell in beside him. One of them mouthed a mocking hiss at Lily—her teeth were filed to points.

"Who are these people, Danny?"

"They're my family." Her face tightened and he reached out to stroke her cheek. "You found yours. I had to find mine. I wish you could have come with me, seen the things I have." He leaned down and kissed her forehead, lips cool and dry. "But I'm glad I got to see you again, before . . . "

"Before what, Danny? What's going on?"

Liquid eyes flickered, glanced away. "I'm leaving. Tomorrow night. I don't think I'm coming back."

Her chest tightened and she caught his hand. "I just found you. Danny, you're in danger."

His smile caught in her throat. "It's not what you think, Lily. It's a good thing. I wish I had time to explain."

The other man shouted over the music, gestured impatiently. "Daniel!"

"I'm sorry," Danny said, squeezing her hand. "I have to go. It was good to see you."

And he turned and followed his friends, disappearing into the press. Lily followed, but found only writhing strangers and dizzying lights.

"Do you really think you can save him?" the witch asked. Fabric rasped as she leaned back against the cushions.

"I'm the only one who'll even try." Shadows and incense filled Lily's head, dizzied her. The air was too thick, cloying on her tongue. "I'm the only one he has."

"What if he doesn't want to be saved?" Lily's jaw tightened and she looked away. Gethsemane laughed, rich as opium.

"Will you help me or not?"

"You're clever, clever and brave. Foolish too, but time may cure that. I can help you. I can tell you where to find your brother, give you what you'll need to go there and return alive."

"What do you want?"

"Service."

"Service. What kind of service?"

"Any kind I ask for." Black lips curved. "You'll give me your name, and you'll work for me. Little things, mostly—running errands, fetching and carrying, traveling. And someday I'll ask you to do something you don't want to, something you'll hate, that will make you hate yourself. You'll curse me, and yourself, and your brother. And you'll do it anyway. That is the price of my help."

Down and down and down, and the walls narrow and tighten around her. She can't see, can't breathe. Not enough air, only dust and dark and cold, filling her chest and choking her. Dirt coats her hands and face, sweat and tears tracking runnels of slime.

Her hands bleed from a dozen falls, back and breasts bruised from squeezing through cracks. The flashlight is gone; she's not sure when she lost it. Colors swim through the darkness.

He needs you.

Their mother lost herself in the twists and turns of her own mind, lost herself so deep she could only find her way out with pills and a razor. Danny found his own labyrinth.

Bile sears her throat, but she swallows it down and keeps moving. She reaches into her shirt, pulls out the amulet the witch gave her, the strange star-sigil. For protection, she said. Cold and slick against her fingers, something real, some reminder that this isn't all a nightmare.

If only it was. Just a dream, and she would wake up in her

own bed and there would be no witch, no bargains, no strange tunnels worming beneath a strange city.

But this hurts too much to be a dream.

The nightmare was an old one.

Lily climbed the steps to their cheap rented rooms, dread like icewater in her stomach. She knew what was coming, always knew in the dream, but she could never stop her dream-self, never keep sixteen-year-old Lily from rushing up the creaking stair. Dream-Lily only knew that something was wrong, that Danny was scared and crying.

She'd only been gone a few hours, such a tiny piece of time stolen for herself. They would leave soon, like they always left when the voices in her mother's head got too loud, warning of some danger she could never explain. It would have been so easy to disappear, to pack a bag and leave when her mother passed out with whatever she was taking to keep the voices quiet that week. But Danny wouldn't leave, and Lily couldn't leave Danny.

So she ran up the stairs, heart pounding with Danny's fear, opened the door to find her brother huddled in the corner, rain leaking through a cracked window and puddling on the floor.

No. It had been sunny that day. Bright and warm. The heat had made the smell worse.

Dream-Lily turned, saw the bathroom door ajar. She sucked in a breath, tasted copper and something cloying and sickly-sweet. In the dream it smelled like roses and incense, instead of blood and shit.

She pushed the door open slowly, hinges squealing, until

she saw the first splatter of blood on yellowed linoleum.

And Lily woke crying, in the darkness of a different city, a different cheap room. Not again. Not again.

Rain rushed through the gutters outside. She huddled on the bed, stared at the cracked window and waited for morning.

Light. She doesn't believe it at first, just a trick of her straining eyes, but it doesn't go away. A cold yellow flicker lining the bottom of a door, bright as neon after so much dark. She moves closer, hears a soft susurrus of voices. She wants to feel relief at this break from silent black, but it only twists the dread deeper.

The door is metal-bound wood, worn dark and shiny with age and oil. Lily scrubs a hand over her face, wipes dirt and tears and mucous onto her pants. She touches the amulet again, and the weight of the knife inside her jacket. Its shape is bruised into her ribs. A wicked little thing with a curved black blade. *It severs bindings*, the witch said as she pressed the hilt into Lily's hand.

Her stomach cramps, and she's glad she hasn't eaten today. Fear fills her belly instead. The links of the necklace bite into her palm and she forces her hand to unclench.

The door is locked. Her knock echoes through the wood, reverberates off stone. The voices pause, and footsteps draw closer.

"*Kdo tam?*" a man's voice asks, and Lily can barely remember English, let alone Czech, so she knocks again.

The door swings open a few inches, and a man's backlit head appears in the gap. The man from the club. His face is shadowed, but she imagines his frown, hears it in his voice. "Co si přejete?"

Her mouth is dry, gritty with dust. "I'm here for Daniel."

The door opens wider, spilling light over half his face. Heavy eyebrows draw together. "He is ours now."

Lily raises her bleeding hand. "I have the prior claim."

His frown deepens as he stares at her. "I see. Come in, then."

He stands aside and Lily steps into the sodium-yellow gloom. Goosebumps crawl over her skin and she clenches her teeth to stop their chattering. Murmurs chase each other around the room as she enters, too low for her to understand.

People stand against the walls of the vaulted room. Lily's not sure what she expected after Gethsemane's cautions—robes and chanting, maybe, hooded assassins with black knives. But they're young, ordinary. She would have passed them on the street in a dozen cities and never looked twice. The leopard girls are there, standing beside a stone plinth in the center where Danny lies. They give way as she approaches, wild eyes following her.

"You shouldn't have followed me here," Danny murmurs as she crouches beside him.

"Please, Danny. I'm sorry I didn't come sooner. I'm sorry I let you go."

He wipes away muddy tear tracks on her face. "It's okay. I found where I needed to be."

She presses her scabbing hand to his chest, trying not to wince as she touches the tattoo. "You belong with your family."

"This is my family now, Lily." He covers her hand with his. Scabs split, smear blood across the ink.

"Come with me, Danny."

He shakes his head, that bemused little smile curving his lips. "I can't leave. I'm going tonight, going to the angels."

"What do you mean?"

"He means," a new voice cuts in, "that you've come too late." A man steps out of the shadows, leather coat flapping around his ankles. He speaks softly, but his voice echoes, shivers through the roots of Lily's teeth. She can't see his face. Shadows and light slide off him, want nothing to do with him.

Something glints in his hand—a straight razor. Lily's stomach clenches. Just like the one her mother used. She tenses, ready to dodge, but he lays the blade on the plinth beside Danny.

"Your brother traveled a long way after you left him, a long way to find us. Tonight he'll travel farther still."

She lets go of Danny's hands, stands to face the man, but his eyes are full of stars and she can't meet his gaze. *He left me*, she thinks, but she won't defend herself to this unnerving stranger. "What have you done to him?"

"We've taken care of him, gave him a family when he had no one else. In return, he's going to help us build a bridge."

His voice rattles in her head like wasps, all pricking feet and buzzing wings, stingers poised. The room spins in a nauseous swirl of yellow and black and she sways . . .

Her hand closes over the necklace, silver cold and clean against her palm. The insects vanish, the dizziness subsides. Lily sucks in a deep breath, but the man's scent fills her nose, coats her tongue. He smells like altars, dust and bone, wine and frankincense and bitter myrrh. She fights the urge to spit.

"What do you mean, a bridge?"

"A bridge to heaven. A bridge of his blood, of his soul."

She glances at Danny; he's holding the razor, staring at the shining steel. "Put that down." But he doesn't listen.

"Daniel didn't tell us his sister was a twin." The man steps forward. "This could make the bridge even stronger." He reaches out with one long hand and freezes, breath hissing through his teeth. He looks at the necklace in Lily's hand.

"So. You're already claimed."

The fountain pen warmed in Lily's hand as she stared at the page in front of her. Other names lay in neat lines at the top, but she couldn't read them in the flickering light. She stared at the blank line, the thick paper.

For Danny.

She thought her hand would shake too much to write, but when nib touched paper her trembling stilled. Ink dark as blood, smooth strong lines as she traced the familiar loops and whorls of her name. She paused for an instant at the end, and liquid black feathered through the fibers of the page.

Gethsemane smiled, sharp and cold as a razor. "It's done. Welcome to the family, Lillian."

Lily shivered at the weight of her name on the woman's tongue. "Now tell me how to find my brother."

"Of course." Black eyes held Lily's. "Listen carefully."

"I won't have anything to do with you, and neither will Danny."

The man looks at her with those star-filled eyes and she tries not to flinch. "Daniel has made his own decisions. Your claim is worthless now. But you can still join your brother, join us. I can even protect you from whomever it was you were foolish enough to bargain with."

She turns away, dizzy from watching him. Danny stares at her with liquid eyes. "You can stay with us, Lily. Stay with me."

If she'd only argued harder, if she'd only gone with him like he asked . . . His heartbeat echoes hers, and she feels the drug-induced languor that suffuses him. She wants to melt into it, let it wash her clean. She squeezes her left hand shut, spilling pain up her arm. Danny winces.

"Do you really mean it?" Her voice cracks. "Do you choose them?"

His eyes sag shut. He's floating in warmth, warmth that takes the pain out of choices. "I do. I don't need you to save me anymore."

"Daniel—" The man's voice shivers through the air. "The stars are setting. We've wasted enough time already."

"Right . . . "

The watchers move closer, link hands to form a circle. Lily's skin prickles with static. A chant picks up, soft sing-song nonsense syllables that set her head throbbing. The razor gleams in Danny's hand.

"No!" Lily tries to grab him, but the doorman is there, pinning her arms, holding her back.

Danny gasps as the razor bites, and Lily echoes it. Steel parts skin and meat, finds the vein. He jerks it down, from elbow to wrist; their mother taught them how to do it right.

Blood spills black as ink, a rush of liquid shadows, and the smell of sweet pennies fills the air. Lily screams and goes limp in her captor's arms.

Only the ghost of pain, only the flood of warmth. Tears slide hot down Lily's face, fill her mouth with salt. Danny raises the blade again, but his hand is slippery and shaking and the second cut is shallow and awkward. It doesn't matter—it'll get the job done.

The doorman lets Lily go, and she collapses onto the dirty floor. She can't feel the cold anymore, just the warm wetness, the pulse of life rushing out of her.

"Your arrival is luckier than I would have imagined, actually," the star-eyed man says, standing over her. His voice is nearly lost under the chanting. "The bond between you and your brother will make the bridge more stable. You brother dies, you live, and the way is opened."

The knife in her jacket presses into her chest. And Lily knows what to do. She pushes herself to her knees, draws the blade. The pocket rips with a snarl of leather and nylon.

"What do you think you can do with that?" the man asks.

She rips her shirt open, snapping buttons. Goosebumps prickle her chest as she bares the birthmark. "Sever bindings." And she drags the blade across her skin, bisecting the mark. Blood trickles down her ribs, soaks into her pants. Not very deep; deep enough.

A sound like a broken guitar string reverberates in her head. For an instant she's blind and deaf. Senses return, except for one, except for Danny. She staggers to her feet, an echoing empty space inside her where her brother used to be.

Danny's eyes widen as he feels it too. Blood pools on the

stone bench, washes onto the floor. Lily stares at the gaping wounds, but all she can feel is her own bruised and scraped skin.

"What did you do?" Danny asks, voice slurring. His eyes are dimming beneath the glaze, spine bowing with the effort of sitting up.

"I set myself free." She stumbles toward him, falls to her knees. "Oh, Danny, I'm so sorry." Nothing the witch could ever ask will be so bad. Nothing can make her hate herself more than this.

"S'okay," he mumbles, and his head falls onto her shoulder. "My choice . . . "

"I know." And she drives the knife up, through the twisting yellow sign on his heart, through the twin-mark it obscures. He makes a wet choking sound and convulses against her. For once the only pain she feels is her own.

Lily twists the blade, and sets him free.

The chorus breaks into screams. She drops Danny's body onto the bloody stone and rises, knife held dripping in front of her. One of the leopard girls collapses writhing to the floor. The other kneels beside her, nose leaking black blood. Lily whirls toward the doorman, but he's on his knees clutching his head. Her other hand grips the amulet as she backs toward the door.

The star-eyed man glares at her and hisses. Maybe he'll kill her, and the witch will lose after all. But instead he vanishes in a twist of nothing, an ear-popping shudder that shakes the room. She shakes off curses and grasping hands and runs, back into the hungry darkness.

———

Easier if the labyrinth simply ate her, but it doesn't. She crawls back, bleeding and bruised and numb, back to the real world. She crawls back to the witch, who waits with her twisting ink and cold smiles.

Gethsemane touches Lily's cheek, and the gentleness of her fingers is worse than any blow. "Welcome home, Lillian."

Cat Rambo lives and writes in the Pacific Northwest in a household consisting of her charming spouse Wayne and two cats, Raven and Taco. Her work has appeared in Fantasy Magazine, Strange Horizons, *and* Subterranean, *among other places. She is a graduate of the Johns Hopkins Writing Seminars and Clarion West 2005.*

"Sugar" was, in fact, inspired by the great pirate story rush of early '07, but Sean took it before I could submit it to any of the anthologies. It's set south of the seaport of Tabat, on the New Continent—the same world as many of my stories as well as the novel I'm currently working on. It started with the image of the worker golems lined up before their sorceress-mistress and grew from there.

SUGAR

Cat Rambo

They line up before Laurana, forty baked clay heads atop forty bodies built of metal cylinders. Every year she casts new heads to replace those lost to weather, the wild, or simple erosion. She rarely replaces the bronze cylinders of their bodies. They are scuffed and battered, over a century old.

Every morning, the island sun beating down on her scalp, she stands on the maison's porch with the golems before her. Motionless. Expressionless.

She chants. The music and the words fly into the clay heads

and keep them thinking. The golems are faster just after they have been charged. They move more lightly, with more precision. With more joy. Without the daily chant they could go perhaps three days at most, depending on the heaviness of their labors.

This month is cane-planting season. She delegates the squads of laborers and sets some to carrying buckets from the spring to water the new cane shoots while others dig furrows. The roof needs reshingling, but it can wait until planting season is past. As the golems shuffle off, she pauses to water the flowering bushes along the front of the house, knowing that the scent will drift into Britomart's sick chamber. Placing her fingertips together, she conjures a tiny rain cloud, wringing moisture from the air. Warm drops collect on the leaves, rolling down to darken pinkish-gray bark to black.

Inside, the house is quiet. The three servants are in the kitchen, cooking breakfast and gossiping. She comes up to the doorway like a ghost, half fearing what she will hear. Nothing but small, inconsequential things. Jeanette says when she takes her freedom payment, she will ask for a barrel of rum, and then go sell it in the street, three silver pieces a cup, over at Sant Tigris, the pirate city. She has a year to go in the sorceress' service.

Daniel has been here a year and has four more to go. He is still getting used to the golems, still eyes them warily when he thinks no one can see him. He is thin and wiry, and his face is pockmarked and scarred by the Flame Plague. He was lucky to escape the Old Country with his life. Lucky to live here now, and he knows it.

Tante Isabelle has been with her since the cook was a girl

of thirteen. Now she's eighty-five, frail as one of the butter-flies that move through the bougainvillea. A black beak's snap, and the butterfly will be gone. She sits peeling cubes of ginger, which she will boil with sugar and lime juice to make sweet syrup that can flavor tea or conjured ice.

"If you sell rum, everyone will think you are selling what lies between your thighs as well!" she says, eying Jeanette.

Jeanette shrugs and tosses her head. "Maybe I'd make even more that way!" she says, ignoring Daniel's blush.

Tante Isabelle looks up to see Laurana standing there. The old woman's smile as she spies her mistress is sweet as sunshine, sweet as sugar. Laurana stands in the doorway, and the three servants smile at her, as they always do, at their beautiful mistress. No thought ever crosses their minds of betraying or displeasing her. It never occurs to them to wonder why.

Christina is a pirate. She wears bright calicos stolen from Indian traders and works on a ship that travels in lazy shark-like loops around the Lesser and Greater Southern Isles, looking for strays from the Aztec treasure fleet and Dutch merchants. The merchants prey on impoverished colonies, taking their entire crops in return for food and tools. The Aztec treasure fleet is part of a vast corrupt network, fed by springs of gold. This is what Christina tells Laurana, how she justifies her profession of blood and watery death.

When Christina comes to Sant Tigres, she goes to the inn and sends one of the pigeons the innkeeper keeps on the roof. It flies to Laurana's window, and she leaves her maison to sail to the port in a small skiff, standing all the way from one island to the other, sea winds whipping around her. She focuses her will and asks the air sylphs, with whom she does not normally converse, to bear her to her lover's scarlet and orange clad arms.

Tiny golden hoops, each set with a charm created by Laurana, are set in Christina's right ear. One is a tiny glass fish, protection against drowning, and another a silver lightning bolt, to ward off storms.

Christina likes to order large meals when she comes ashore. Her crew hunts the unsettled islands and catches the wild cattle and hogs so abundant there to eke out their income. The pirates sell the excess fat and hides to the exiles and smugglers that fill these islands. So she is not meat-starved now, but wants sugary treats, confections of butter and sweet, washed down with raw swallows of rum, here in harbor, where she can be safely drunk.

"Pretty farmer," she says now. She touches the sorceress's hair, which was black as Christina's once, but which has gone silver with age, despite her unlined skin and her clear, brilliant blue eyes.

"Pretty pirate," Laurana replies, feeling the familiar tug of disloyalty at the words. She spends the evening buying drinks for Christina and her crew. The pirates count on her deep pockets, rich with gold from selling sugar. Sometimes they try to sell her things plundered on their travels, ritual components or scrolls or trinkets laden with spells. The only present Christina ever brought her was a waxed and knotted cord strung with knobby, pearly shells. Laurana hung it on her bedchamber wall where the full moon's light can polish it each month.

Laurana brings Christina presents: fresh strawberries

and fuzzy nectarines from her greenhouse. In Sant Tigres, she trades sugar for bushels of chocolate beans and packets of spices. Someday, when circumstances have changed, she would like Christina to spend a day or two at the plantation. Jeannette would outdo herself with the meals, flakey pastries and flowers of spun sugar.

Past time to send for a new cook, she thinks. It will take a few months to post the message and then for the new arrival to appear, and even more time for Jeannette to train her in the ways of the kitchen and how to tell the golems to fetch and carry.

Someone leans forward to ask her a question. It is a new member of Christina's crew, curious about the rumors of her plantation.

"Human slaves are doomed to failure," she says. "Look what happened on Banbur—discontented servants burned the fields and overtook the town there, turning their masters and mistresses out into the underbrush or setting them to labor."

"And," she added. "Whites do badly in this climate. I can take care of myself and my household, but it is easier to not worry about my automatons growing ill or dying."

Although they did die, after a fashion. They wore away, their features blurred with erosion. They cracked and crumbled— first the noses, then the lips and brows, their eyes becoming pitted shadows, their molded hair a mottling of cracks.

Beyond replacing the cook, she would redecorate. She did it every few decades. She would send a letter and eventually a company representative would show up, consult with her, and then sail away, to be replaced by new wallpaper and carpets, sets of china and porcelain wash basins. She looks at Christina and pictures her against blue silk sheets, olive skin gleaming in candle glow.

Later they fall into bed together and she stays there for two hours before she rises, despite her lover's muffled, sleepy protests, and takes her skiff back to her own island. Overhead the sky is a black bowl set with glittering layers of stars, grainy as sandstone and striated with light. Moonlight dapples the waves, so dark and impenetrable that they look like stone.

At home, she goes upstairs. A passage cuts across the house, running north to south to take advantage of the trade wind, and the room partitions are set with open squares at the top to let the wind through. Britomart's is the northern-most room.

The air smells of dawn and sugar. Sugar, sweet and translucent as Britomart's skin, the color of snow drifts, laid on cool white linen. The other woman's ivory hair, which matches Laurana's, is spread out across the pillow.

Tonight her face is unmasked, though normally she spares the rest of the household the sight of it. Laurana does not flinch away from the pitted eyes, the face more eroded than any golem's. Outside in the courtyard, the black and white deathbirds hop up and down in the branches, making the crimson flowers shake in the early morning light.

"Pleasant trip?" Britomart says.

Laurana's answer is noncommittal. Sometimes her old lover is kind, but she is prone to lashing out in sudden anger. Laurana does not blame her for that. Her death is proving neither painless nor particularly short, but it is coming, nonetheless. A month? A year? Longer? Laurana isn't sure.

How long have they been locked in this conversation? It has been less than six months so far, she knows, but it seems like forever.

She goes to her room. The bed is turned down and a hot brick has been slipped between the sheets to warm them. A bouquet of ginger sits on the table near the lamp, sending out its bold perfume.

She lies in bed and fails to sleep. Britomart's face floats before her in the darkness. She is unsure if she is dreaming or really seeing it. She wonders if she remembers it as worse than it really is. But she doesn't.

Two weeks later, the pigeon at her window.

Christina has a bandage around her upper arm, nothing much, she says, carelessness in a battle. She pushes Laurana away, though apologetically. Rather than sleep together, they stay awake and talk. It is their first conversation of any length.

"So she's sick, your friend?" Christina says.

"You were raised here in the islands," Laurana answers. "You don't know what it was like in the Old Country. In the space of three years, sorcerers destroyed two continents. Everyone decided to make their power play at once. They called dragons up out of the earth and set them killing. The Flame Plague moved from town to town. Entire villages went up like candles. Millions died, and the earth itself was charred and burned, magic stripped from it. Some fought with elementals, and others with summoned winds and fogs, but others with poisoned magics."

She pours herself more wine. Christina's skin is paler than

usual, but the lantern light in the room gleams on it as though it were flower petals.

"And you were here . . . " Christina prompts.

"I was here in the islands, preparing to go. I heard that Britomart had blundered into someone else's trap and was dying of it, being eaten away. I brought her down. The magic is clean here, and there are serendipities and artifacts. I hoped to heal her."

"But that hasn't happened."

The wine is mulled with cinnamon and clove and sugar that has not completely dissolved, a gritty sweet residue at the cup's bottom.

"No," she says. "That hasn't happened."

Christina smuggles Laurana onto her ship while it's at harbor. She and three other sailors are supposed to be watching it. Laurana sits with them drinking shots of rum until the yellow moon swings itself up over the prow, its face broad and grinning as a baby's. It reminds her of Britomart and she feels her tears well up. She savors the moment, for magic removes almost all capacity to weep.

She nudges Christina and points to the distant reef. Out on the rocks, mermaids cluster, fishy eyes shining in the moonlight, fleshy gills pulsing like tidepool creatures shuttered close by the light. She kisses Christina as they watch

Eventually, the two climb into Christina's bunk.

She leaves in the small hours, past the stares of the mermaids. It is still planting season and the golems work day and night.

When she first came to the island she tried yellow-flowered

sea-island cotton. Then indigo and ginger. With the arrival from the Wizard's College of Tabat, sending out the results of the Duke's experiments, of schematics for three-roller mills and copper furnace pots, sugar cane has become the crop of choice. Her workers perform the day and night labor that must be undertaken when the cane is harvested, transmuting it into sugar and molasses. She makes rum too, and ships barrels of it along with the molasses casks and thick cones of molded muscovado sugar to Sant Tigres, which consumes or trades all she can supply.

Most sorcerers are not strong enough to animate so many golems. She has the largest plantation in this area. Others, though, have followed her lead, although on a smaller scale. It took decades for them to realize how steadily she was making money, despite the depredations of the Dutch merchants or the pirates they paid to disrupt the Aztec shipping trade.

She had been to the Old Country before all the trouble, two years learning science at a school, where she had met Britomart, who was an actual princess as well as a sorceress. Laurana had been centuries old when she met Britomart but she had dared to hope that here was her soul mate, the person who would stay by her side over all the centuries to come.

But in the end, she wanted to return to her island, full of new techniques and machineries that she thought would improve the yield. Rotating fields and planting those lying fallow with clover, to be plowed into the soil to enrich it for planting. Plans for a windmill to be built to the southeast, facing into the wind channeled through the mountains, with sails made of wooden frames tied with canvas. Lenses placed together that allowed one to observe the phases of heaven and the moons that surrounded other planets, and the accompanying elegant Copernican theories to explain their movements.

She swore to Britomart that she would return by the next rainy season. She kept her promise.

But by then, the trap had been sprung and Britomart had begun to rot away, victim of a magic left by a man who had died two weeks previously.

"You're ready to be rid of me," Britomart says.

"Of course not."

"It's true, you are!"

She goes about the room, conjuring breezes and positioning them to blow across the bed's expanse.

"You are," Britomart whispers. "I would be."

Two breezes collide at the center of the bed. Britomart wants it cold, ever colder. It slows the decay, perhaps. Laurana isn't sure of that either.

Outside she sees that the golems are nearly done with the south-east field. One more to go after that. She glances over the building, tallying up the things to be done. Roof. Trimming back the bushes. Exercising the horse she had thought Britomart would ride.

Half a mile away is the beach shore. Her skiff is pulled up there, tied to a rock. Standing beside it, she can see the smudge of Sant Tigres on the horizon.

She is so tired that she aches to her bones. Somewhere deep inside her, she is aware, there is an endless well of sorrow, but she is simply too weary to pay it any mind. It is one of the peculiarities of mages that they can compartmentalize themselves, and put away emotions to never be touched again.

She does this now, rousing herself, and prepares to go on. She has a pact with the universe, which told her long ago when she became a sorceress: *nothing will be asked that cannot be endured.* So she soldiers on like her workers, marching through the days.

She is still tired, months later.

"Go to her," Britomart says. "I don't care. You don't have much time with her."

"I have even less with you," Laurana says, but Britomart still turns away.

It is harvesting season. Outside in the evening, some of the golems are in the boiling house, where three boilers sit over the furnace, cooking the sugar cane sap. The syrup passes from boiler to boiler until in the last it begins to crystallize into muscovado. Two golems pack it into clay sugar molds and set the molds in the distillery so the molasses will drain away.

In the distillery, more golems walk across the mortar and cobble floor in which copper cauldrons are set for molasses collection, undulating channels feeding them the liquid.

They mix cane juice into the brew before casking it. In a few months, it will be distilled into fiery, raw rum and sold to the taverns in the pirate city.

She goes and fetches her notebook and sits in the room with Britomart, her pen scratching away to record the day's labors, the number of rows harvested, and making out a list of necessities for her next trip to Sant Tigres. She estimates two thousand pounds of sugar this year, three hundred casks of molasses, and another two hundred of rum. Recently she received word that the sorcerer Carnuba, whose plantation is three days south, renovated his sugar mill to process lime juice. Lime juice is an excellent scurvy preventative, and much in demand—she wonders how long it would take a newly planted grove to fruit. Her pen dances across the page, calculating raw material costs and the best forms of transportation.

"Is she pretty?" Britomart asks. Her face is still turned away.

Laurana considers. "Yes," she says.

"As pretty as I was?" The anguish in the whisper forces Laurana to put down her pen. She takes Britomart's hands in hers. They are untouched by the disease, the nails sleek and shiny and well-groomed. Hands like the necks of swans, or white doves arcing over the gleam of water.

"Never that pretty," she says.

The next morning, Laurana goes through the room, touching each charm to stillness until the lace curtains no longer flutter. Until there is no sound in the room except her own breathing and the warbling calls of the deathbirds clustering among the blossoms of the bougainvillea tree outside.

She hears a fluttering from her room, a pigeon that has joined the dozen others on the windowsill, but she ignores it, as she ignored the earlier arrivals. She sits beside the bed, listening, listening. But the figure on the bed does not take another breath, no matter how long she listens.

All through that day, the golems labor boiling sugar. Jeanette brings her lemonade and the new girl, Madeleine, has made biscuits. She drinks the sweet liquid and looks at the dusty wallpaper. The thought of changing it stuns her with the energy it would require. She will sit here, she thinks, until she dies, and dust will collect on her and the wallpaper alike.

Still, when dinner-time comes she goes downstairs and under Tante Isabelle's watchful eye, she pushes some food around on her plate.

Daniel cannot help but be a little thankful that Britomart is dead, she thinks. He was the one who emptied her chamber pot and endured her abuse when she set him to fetching and carrying. The thought makes her speak sharply to him as he serves the chowder the new girl has made. He looks bewildered by her tone and slinks away. She regrets the moment as soon as it is passed but has no reason for calling him back.

Upstairs the ranks of the pigeons have swollen by two or three more. She lies on her bed, fully clothed, and stares at the ceiling.

The next morning two golems carry Britomart's body for her. They dig the grave on a high slope of the mountain, overlooking the bay. It is a fine view, she thinks. One Britomart would have liked.

When they have finished, she stands with her palms turned upwards to the sky, calling clouds to come seething on the wind. They collect, darkening like burning sugar. When they are at the perfect, furious boil, she brings lightning down from them to smash the stone that stands over the grave. She does it over and over again, carving Britomart's name in deep and angry, blackened letters.

At home she goes to lie in bed again.

One by one, the golems grind to a stop at their labors, and the sap boils over in thick black smoke. They stand wherever their energy gave out, but all manage in their last moments to bring their limbs in towards their torsos, standing in stalky stillness.

It may be the smoke that draws Christina. She arrives, knocks on the door, and comes inside, brushing past the servants. Without knowing the house, she manages to come upstairs and to Laurana's bedroom.

Laurana does not move, does not look over at the door.

Christina comes to the bed and lies down beside the sorceress. She looks around at the bedroom, at the string of shells hanging on the wall, but says nothing. She strokes Laurana's ivory hair with a soft hand until the tears begin.

Outside the golems grind to life again as the rain starts. They collect the burned vats and trundle them away. They cask the most recent rum and set the casks on wooden racks to ferment. They put the plantation into order, and finish the last of their labors. Then as the light of day fades, muffled by the steady rain, they arrange themselves again, closing themselves away, readying for tomorrow.

Holly Phillips lives in the mountains of western Canada. She is a full-time writer, with two books in print—her award-winning collection In the Palace of Repose *and her first novel,* The Burning Girl—*and another novel,* Engine's Child, *due to appear from Del Rey in 2008. Holly is also co-editing the Canadian SF anthology* Tesseracts 11 *with Cory Doctorow. About "Brother of the Moon" she says: "This story was, in a small way, inspired by the forces of history we see moving all around us. Canada is a pretty safe backwater, but it seems important to remember all the places in the world where history rolls over people's lives like a bulldozer."*

BROTHER OF THE MOON

Holly Phillips

Our hero wakes in his sister's bed. Last night's vodka drains through him in sluggish ebb, leaving behind the silt of hangover, the unbrushed taste of guilt. He rolls onto his stomach, feeling the rumpled bed wallow a little on the last of the alcoholic waves, and opens his eyes. His sister sleeps with her curtains open. The tall window across from the bed is brilliant with a soft spring sunlight that slips past crumbled chimneys and ornate gables to shine on his sister's hands. She has delicate little monkey's paws, all tendon and brittle bone, that look even more fragile than usual edged by the morning light. Sitting cross-legged among the rumpled sheets, touch as an underfed orphan in the undershirt and sweatpants she uses as pajamas, our hero's sister is flipping a worn golden coin. She is a princess. Our hero is a prince.

The coin sparkles in a rising and falling blur. Our hero watches with bemusement and pleasure as his sister's nimble hands catch the coin, display the winning face, send it spinning and winking through sunlight with the flick of a thumb. Our hero's sister manipulates the coin, a relic of ancient times, with a skill our hero would never have guessed. It is the skill of a professional gambler who could stack a deck of cards in her sleep, which is mystifying. Our hero's sister is not the gambling type. Our hero clears a sour vodka ghost from his throat.

"You're up early."

The coin blinks at him and drops into his sister's hand. With her fingers closed around it, she leans over him and kisses his stubbled head.

"You snore."

"I don't," he says. "Are you winning?"

"It keeps coming up kings." Her monkey's hands toy with the coin, teasing the golden sunshine into our hero's eyes. "Who were you with last night?"

Our hero scrubs his tearing eyes with a fold of her sheet. The linen is soft and yellow with age and smells of his sister. "No one special. No one. I forget."

His sister's face is like her hands, delicate, bony, feral. Our hero thinks she's beautiful, and loves her with the conscious, deliberate tenderness of someone who has lost every important thing but one.

"How do you know I snore?" he says. "You're the woman who can sleep through bombs."

This is literal truth. When the New Army was taking the city and the two of them were traveling behind the artillery line, she had proven she could sleep through anything. But she says, "Bombs don't steal the covers," and since our hero is lying on top of the blanket, fully dressed, with his shod feet hanging off the end of the bed, he understands that she was awakened by something other than him. It troubles him that he cannot guess what might have been troubling her. Or perhaps it is a deeper worry, that he can imagine what it might have been. He stretches out a hand and steals the coin from between her fingers. The gold is as warm and silky as her skin. The face of the king has been the same for five hundred years.

"Granddad," our hero says ironically.

His sister sighs and stretches out beside him, stroking his head.

"You need to shave," she says.

People have said they are too close. The new government has cited rumors of incest as one reason to edge our hero out of the public eye. The rumors are false, they have never been lovers. But perhaps it is more honest to say that if they are lovers, they have always been chaste. She rubs her palm back and forth across his scalp, and he knows how much she enjoys the feel of stubble just long enough to bend from prickly to soft, because he enjoys it so much himself. Her touch soothes his headache and he is on the verge of dropping off when a van mounted with loudspeakers rolls by in the narrow street below, announcing the retreat of the New Army—the new New Army, our hero thinks, remembering all the friends and rivals who have died—routed from the border in the south.

The invasion has begun. Our hero squints to see the losing face of the coin against the mounting sun. The tree and moon of the vanished kingdom has been smoothed into clouds by generations of uncrowned monarchs' hands.

"One toss," our hero's sister says across the echoes of the retreating van. "If it comes up moons, I'll go."

Dread knots his stomach, but he does as she asks. She is the only person in the world he will obey, not because she rules him, but because he trusts her when he does not himself know what is right. This is often the case these days. Maybe there are no more rights left. Maybe there are only lesser wrongs. He props his head on his fist and flips the coin, catching it in his cupped palm. Moons. He makes a fist before his sister can see, and feels as if he is clenching his hand around his own heart. It's a dreadful duty, a calamity whichever one of them goes, but he would rather be lost than lose her. Before she can pry his fingers open, he tosses the coin high into the golden light and catches it again with a flourish.

"Kings," he says. She looks at him, stricken, heart-sick, and he is glad of his lie.

Walking north along the river our hero has the road to himself. No one will evacuate in the advent of this war. It is the last war, the death of the independent state, and in any case, Russia and the West have between them closed the borders: there is nowhere to go. Despite the years of infighting and politics, of failing idealism and the gradual debasement of his figurehead's throne, our hero still reflects with nostalgic pride on the romanticism and ruthless practicality of the mercenary army-turned-government he and his sister had fought for, legitimized, defended. They had been conquerors and puppets. They had driven the unlikely alchemy that transformed an imposed dictatorship into the last true democracy in the world. They had been used and pushed aside when they were no longer useful, but they had been loyal. This seems odd to our hero as he walks north along the blue river. He has always put his loyalty in the service of necessity, hidden it behind a guise of practicality, and now he has to wonder what moral force, what instinct of worth has shaped the meaning of need. What need—whose need—sends him north, leaving his sister behind to wait for the end alone? He loves her more than ever, and hates her a little for believing his lie and letting him go.

Walking in the sunshine intensifies his hangover thirst. He feels gritty and unkempt, with a sour gut and a spike through his temples, but his worn army boots hug his feet like old friends, and it is good to be on the move, good to have a destination and a goal. He hopes the security service doesn't give his sister too much grief when they realize he is gone.

There is little traffic after a year of oil embargoes. There are pedestrians, a few horse carts, peasant working their fields with mattock and hoe. Peasants who will watch the invasion on satellite feed, who will email reports to relatives in Frankfurt and London and Montreal, who will tell one another with pride and a languorous despair that they are sticking it out to the end. A young man wearing a billed cap with the logo of an American sports team dips his hand into the bag slung across his back and casts his seed with a sweeping gesture, a generous, open-handed gesture that answers the question *why* with a serene and simple *because*. He pauses between casts to raise his hand to our hero passing on the road. Our hero answers with an abbreviated wave and turns his head away, afraid of being recognized, afraid of being seen with tears in his eyes. Settling into the mud of the ditch between the river and the road lies the burned-out carcass of an army jeep, and there it all is, the present, the future, the past. A blackbird perches on the machine gun mount and sings its three note song. It is an image with all the solace of a graveyard.

Our hero walks off his hangover and an old vitality begins to well up through the sluggish residue left by weeks, months, of dissolution. He has relaxed into the journey, and the bolt of adrenaline he suffers when he sees the checkpoint ahead feels like a sudden dose of poison. His stride falters, losing the rhythm of certainty, but he does not stop or turn aside. The checkpoint has of course been sited to give the illegitimate traveler minimum opportunities for escape. He has papers, but he is afraid of being the victim of love or hate. He tells himself he is only afraid of being stopped, but does not believe his own lie.

The soldiers are young, volunteers in the new New Army, dressed in flak jackets and running shoes and jeans. One of them is a woman. She is younger than our hero's sister, with blond hair instead of black, brown eyes instead of blue, but she has a solemn, determined self-sufficiency our hero recognizes with a pang, though his sister is much more casual about her courage now. She is more casual about death, both our hero's and her own, and he suspects she has learned to think historically while he still sees the faces of the living and the dead.

Young woman, he thinks at her in a stern Victorian uncle's voice, *you are becoming historical*, which is a joke that would make her smile.

"Where are you going?" the young sergeant asks.

"North," our hero says.

"Away from the border."

This statement is indisputably true. The peacableness with which our hero answers the young people's hostility is not.

"Yes," he says mildly, "I have business there."

"Business." The sergeant's sneer is implicit behind the mask of his face. The bland, deadly façade of a brutal bureaucracy comes naturally to the nation's youth, they have been raised to it. It was the look of freedom that had been, briefly, imposed.

Our hero does not respond to the sergeant's echo. His mouth grows wet with a desire for vodka, and he has a fantasy, rich though fleeting, of walking into the shade of the soldiers' APC with his arm around the young woman's shoulders, hunkering down to pass a bottle around, to educate and uplift them with stories of the Homecoming War. That would be so much better than this. He unbuttons his shirt pocket and takes out his identity papers. The sergeant ignores them.

"We know who you are," he says. "What business can you have away from the capital at such a time?"

This is not an easy question to answer honestly. Our hero does not want to lie, yet claiming an urgent war-related mission in the face of no vehicle, no companions, no standing in the government, is impossible. After too long a silence, our hero says, "I am going to the old capital. It is my ancestral home. I will fight my war from there."

He looks deeply into the sergeant's eyes, and for a moment he thinks the old mystique has come alive, the old ideals of courage, nobility, adventure rising between them like a bridge of understanding, or of hope. But this young man was bred with disillusionment in his bones, and the moment dies.

"Give me your papers," the sergeant says with the blunt and sullen anger of disappointment. "I will have to call it in."

As if she is summoned by his need, Colonel Vronskaya appears with a blast of fury for the recruits and a bottle for our hero. She embraces him with a powerful cushioned grip like a farmwife's, and then stands with her hands clenched on his shoulders to study him the strong spring sun. She is not handsome at close quarters, Martiana Vronskaya. Her eyes are too close-set, too deep-set, too small for her flat, spider-veined face. Our hero leans into her regard, reassured by the familiar hard and humorous clarity of the old New Army, practical, piratical, and oddly moral in her amorality.

"Jesus fuck, you seedy son of a bitch," she says, shaking him. "This is the face we followed to victory?"

"Hell no," our hero says, "but it's the same ass."

"I wish I could say the same."

Vronskaya leads him to her car, a Japanese SUV rigged out in scavenged armor plate, and pulls a bottle of Ukrainian rot-gut from a pocket of her bulging map case. They sit together on the back seat, passing the bottle between them as they talk. The river eases by, blue riffled by white around the ruins of a bridge.

"That river was like a sewer when we came. Shit brown," Vronskaya says, and our hero braces himself for some heavy-handed nostalgia. But his companion stops there, and he feels a youthful apprehension rising through him. He can feel her tension, and knows she is also braced for something hard.

Thinking to make it easier on them both, he nudges her arm with the bottle and says, "You still shooting deserters these days?"

Vronskaya cuts loose with an explosive breath and says, "Hell no, we just kick their asses back to the front."

"It might be easier to tell them to sit down and wait."

"Fuck," Vronskaya says in agreement. She finally takes the bottle and drinks, passes it back. He drinks. She says, "Is that what you're doing? Looking for a good place to wait?"

"Pick your ground and defend it to the end."

"Lousy strategy, my friend. Lousy fucking strategy."

"You have a better one to offer?"

"No."

She drinks. He does. The rotgut burns going down, a welcome heat.

"Go ahead," he says. "Ask your questions."

"What," she says, "you think your crazy sister is the only one who remembers her babya's stories? Okay, okay." He had made a sudden move. "She's not crazy. She's not here, so she's not crazy. But don't tell me this isn't her idea."

"It isn't anyone's idea," our hero says, grandiose with vodka in his veins. "It's fate."

"Sure. Your fate."

"You'd be happy to see us both on this road? You want us both to die?"

"No." Vronskaya speaks with leaden patience. "I don't want you *both* to die."

Our hero slams out of the SUV, startling the checkpoint guards, startling himself. Mindful of weapons in nervous hands he smoothes his hands over his head, feeling the stubble pull at his sunburned scalp. Vronskaya heaves herself out of the car.

"Jesus fuck," she says, "you're serious. You're really going to do this thing."

"If you have any better ideas . . . " our hero says, too tense to give it the right ironic lilt.

"Sure I have better ideas. Fight and die with your old comrades instead of skulking off like a sick dog who's not allowed to die in his mistress's house."

"You never liked her," our hero says.

"No, I never did. Have you ever asked her what she thinks of me? Of any of us?"

"She loves you better than you know," he says, looking into Vronskaya's eyes.

"Me? The country, maybe, I'll grant you that. Me, she doesn't give a shit for, and never has. Or—" But Vronskaya's gaze slips aside.

Or you. But our hero knows that's not true, and knows that Vronskaya knows, so he can let it go. He says, "Will you believe me? This isn't her idea. I was the one who wouldn't let her go."

Vronskaya shrugs, sullen. "So you're the crazy one."

"Maybe. I've always been a gambler, and this is my game to play."

"It's not a game you can fucking win!"

"And yours is? Come on, Martiana, we've already lost. We lost before a shot was fired. You know it, I know it. Those damn kids know it, and so do the soldiers dying in the retreat, and so do the babyas waiting in the capital. We're losing. We've already fucking lost. East and West will meet at the river and swallow us whole." Our hero is shouting, hoarse with years of frustration. Vronskaya, her driver, the checkpoint guards, are all listening with the shame-faced scowl of those caught with their worst fears showing. "We're fucked! We're doomed! *Tell me I'm wrong!*"

In the silence that follows, they can hear a trio of small jets roaring by in the southern sky. The West has promised no civilian populations will be bombed. Even if they keep that promise, everyone knows the Russians won't. Our hero squeezes the back of his neck, then lets his arms fall to his sides.

"I have one card to play, and I'm playing it. What difference does it make where I cash my chips?"

Vronskaya, long-time poker rival, long-time friend, gives him a mournful look and says, "It's bad to die alone."

But our hero won't be alone at the end.

The old capital perches on a high bluff, a forerunner of the northern mountains, like a moth on a wolf's nose. A wing-tattered moth on a grizzled and mangy old half-breed dog, more like, for the hillsides have been logged and grazed, and the ancient town has been starved down to its stony bones. But the river runs deep and fast in a curve around the old walls, white foam clean and bright around sharp-toothed rocks, and the castle high above the slate-roofed town still rears its dark towers against the sky. Jackdaws like winged Gypsies make their livings there. The place might have been a museum once, but now it is not even a ruin, just an empty house with rotten foundations and a badly leaking roof. Our hero and his sister camped there for a time when the New

Army was fighting to reach the modern city on the plain, and he remembers the melancholy ache of nostalgia, the romance of the past and the imperfect conviction that that past was his. But he had been younger then, and dangerous, and he could relish the pain.

The town is quiet. No loudspeakers here, just the murmur of radios and TVs through windows left open on the soft spring evening. It has taken our hero three days to walk this far, but the news is the same. Only the names of the towns marking the army's retreat have changed. His old comrades have managed to slow the invasion some, and along with the sting and throb of his blistered feet and the ache of his empty stomach he feels the burn of the shame he would not admit to Martiana Vronskaya, that he has been walking in the wrong direction. There must be some value to this last mad act. He must somehow make it so.

But how will he know if he has succeeded? The thought of dying in uncertainty troubles him more than the thought of death, and he pauses in his climb up the town's steep streets to sit at an outdoor table of a small café. His feet hurt worse once he is off them and he stretches his legs out to prop them on their heels. A waitress comes out and asks him kindly for his order. She is an older woman and he suspects her of having a son at the front: she is too forgiving of our misplaced hero. She brings him a cup of ferocious coffee and bread and olives and cheese. It all tastes delicious, and he looks up from his plate to tell his sister so, only to be reminded that she is not here. He wishes she was. He would like to see this small, cramped square through her eyes. She notices things: the sparrows waiting for crumbs, the three brass balls above an unmarked door, the carved rainspout jutting a bearded chin over the gutter. These things would tell her something about this neighborhood, this town, this world. To our hero, they are only fragments of an incomprehensible whole. The world is this, and this, and this. It is never complete. It is never done.

Oh God, our hero thinks for the first time, I do not want to die.

His feet hurt worse after the rest and plague him as he climbs the steep upper streets to the castle door. It is an oddly house-like castle, with no outer wall, no courtyard, no barbican and gate. The massive door, oak slabs charred black by the cold smolder of time, stands level with the street, and the long stone of the sill has been worn into a deep smiling curve by the passage of feet. Generations of feet, our hero thinks, an army that has taken a thousand years to pass through this door. The gap between door and sill is wide enough for a cat, but not a child, let alone a man. The sun has fallen below the surrounding roofs and the light has dimmed to a clear, still-water dusk. The stone is a pale creamy gray. The sky is as far as heaven, and blue as his sister's eyes. Our hero, hoping and fearing in equal measure, turns the iron latch and discovers that the door is unlocked. The great wooden weight swings inwards with a whisper of well-oiled hinges, and the boy sitting before the small fire in the very large hearth at the far end of the entrance hall calls out, "Grandfather! He's here!" as if our hero is someone's beloved son returning home. He has no idea who these people are.

The old man and the boy share a name, so they are Old Bradvi and Young Bradvi. They stare at our hero with the same eyes, bright and black and flame-touched, like the tower's birds. Our hero has heard the jackdaws returning to their high nests, their harsh voices unbearably distant and clear through the intervening layers of stone. He remembers that sound, the mournful clarity of the dusk return, and misses his old friends, the lover he had embraced in a cold, cobwebbed room, his sister. He misses her so intensely that her absence becomes a presence, a woman-shaped hole who sits at his side, listening with her eyes on her hands. The boy explains with breathless faith that he and his grandfather have been waiting since the invasion began.

They live in the town. "My mother is there, in our house, watching the television, she wouldn't come, but we have been here all the time."

All the time our hero has been walking, this boy and his grandfather have been here, waiting for him to arrive. Despite himself, our hero feels a stirring of awe, as if his and his sister's despair has given birth to something separate and real.

Old Bradvi says, "Lord, we knew you would come." He makes tea in a blackened pot nestled in the coals, his crow's eyes protected from the smoke by a tortoise's wrinkled lids. In the firelight his face is a wizard's face, and our hero feels as though he has already slipped aside from the world he knows, as though he has already stepped through that final door. When the boy takes up a small electronic game and sends tiny chirps and burbles to echo up against the ceiling, this only deepens the sense of unreality. Or perhaps it is a sense of reality that haunts our hero, the sense that this is the truest hour he has ever lived. The old man pours sweetened tea into a red plastic cup and says, "Lord, it is better to wait until dawn."

Who is this man? How does he know what he knows? Our hero does not ask. Reality weighs too heavily upon him, he has no strength for speculation, and no need for it: they have all been brought here by a story, lured by the same long, rich, fabulous tale that has ruled our hero's life, and that now rules our hero's death. At least the story will go on. Stories have no nations, only hearts and minds, and as long as his people live, there will be those. He drinks his tea and listens beyond the sounds of the fire, the game, the old man's smoker's lungs, to his sister's silent voice.

Late in the night he leaves the old man and the sleeping boy to take a piss. Afterward, he wanders the castle in the dark, finding his way by starlit arrow slits and memory. It is a small castle made to seem larger than it is by its illogical design. It seems larger yet in the darkness, and our hero's memory fails. He stumbles on an unseen stair and sits on cold stone to nurse a bruised shin. He wants to weep in self-pity, and he wants to laugh at the bathos of this moment, this life. He curses softly to the mice, and dozes for a moment with his head on his knee before the chill rouses him again. He climbs the stair, and realizes it is the stair to the tower. The floors are wooden here and there is a cold, complex, living smell of damp oak, bird shit, feathers, smoke. He crosses to a window, his muffled steps rousing sleeping birds above his head, and squeezes himself onto the windowsill. There are few streetlights in the town below, but there are windows bright yellow with lamplight or dimly underwater-blue with TV light. There are lives below those sharp, starlit roofs. There is history out there in the cold, clean air. And there is the moon, a rising crescent that hangs in the night sky no higher than our hero's window, as if it means to look at him eye to eye. A silver blade, a wink, a knowing smile, close enough to tempt his reach, far enough to let him fall if he tried.

Sitting above the town with no company but the moon and the sleeping birds, our hero feels alone, apart, and yet a part of all those lives, all that history taking place right now, here and everywhere, with every beat of every heart. The paradox of loneliness is a black gulf within him, a rift between the broken pieces of his heart. The moon casts his shadow into the room behind him, and there, in the moonlit dark, the shadow of his sister's absence puts her arms around his neck and lays her cheek against his stubbled head, and he turns and leans his face against her breast, wraps his arms about her waist, and finally weeps.

When the stars fade and the frost-colored light of day begins to seep back into the world, the old man brings the knife, and the deed is swiftly done.

It is the birds that wake him. Two jackdaws have drifted down on black wings from the rafters and stand about, peering at him with cocked heads, discussing in sarcastic tones whether he is alive or dead. Dead, he tries to tell them, but his throat remembers the iron blade and closes tight on the word. What is this? he wonders. Is he still dying? But he remembers the knife, the sudden icy tear, the taste of blood, the drowning. Air slides into his lungs at the thought, tasting of dust and feathers. What is this? Is he alive? He sits, clumsy with cold, and the birds sidle off, muttering and unafraid. Their claws make a clock's tock against the floor. Our hero's shirt is stiff and evil with blood. What, then, is this running through his veins? He is too bewildered to feel afraid.

At first he cannot see the changes, and he thinks that he has failed, though how he could have failed and yet be alive escapes him. The dissonance between possibility and impossibility is too intense, he is numb and not, perhaps, entirely sane. He stumbles down the stairs, the same spider-haunted stairs, while the birds leave by the windows. They laugh at him as they go, he has no doubt: jackdaws have a black sense of humor. He blunders his way through the half-remembered halls, gets lost, laughs out of sheer uncomprehending terror. When he finds the entry hall, there is a fire burning on the vast hearth, a whole log alight, filling the fireplace with snapping and dancing flames, but he does not pause. The door is wide open, and the air is bright with morning light, although the sun is still below the roofs of the town.

There are bells ringing somewhere below, a shining tin-tanning of bronze, such a happy sound that our hero pulls off his blood-soaked shirt so as not to sully the good day. He walks bare-chested into the town, and no one stares or looks aside, although the streets are almost crowded. The people are not so happy as the bells; many seem as quietly, profoundly bewildered as our hero feels. He stops a woman about his own age, a woman with soft fair hair tousled across her face, and asks what has happened.

"What do you mean?" she says. "Everything has happened. Everything!"

"O God," an older woman says beside them. "O God, do not abandon us. O God, preserve us."

A man across the narrow street is cursing with a loud and

frantic edge to his voice. He seems to be haranguing his car which is parked with two wheels up on the pavement, and which is no doubt out of gas after all these months of the embargo. Our hero supposes that the invading armies are near, perhaps at the fragile old walls of the town, and so, although there is something odd about the man's defunct automobile, he continues on down the hill toward the river where he might be able to see what there is to see.

But there are other odd things, and gradually they begin to distract him from the shock of being alive. The streets are wider as they near the archaic boundary of the old wall, and the pavements here are lined with strange statues. Wrought-iron coaches with weighty and elaborate ornaments, brass lions with blunt, dog-like faces and curling manes, horses with legs like pistons and gilded springs. The people clustered around these peculiar artworks are predictably confused, but there are others in the streets who walk with shining eyes and buoyant steps, and some of these people, too, seem odd to our hero. Their clothing is too festive, their hair is strung with baubles, their faces are at once laughing and fierce. One bearded man catches our hero's eye and bows. He sweeps off his jacket, blue velvet stiff with gold braid, and offers it to our hero with another bow. "My lord," he says, and when our hero takes what is offered, the man spreads his arms with a wide flourish, as if to present to him everything: the people, the town, the world.

And then our hero sees, as if before he had been blind. The tired old houses propped up by silver barked trees hung with jewel-faceted fruit. The banners lazily unfurling from lampposts that have moonstones in place of glass. The violets shivering above the clear, speaking stream that runs down the gutter, between the clawed feet of the transformed cars. It is the new world, the ancient world, the world that had faded to a golden dream on the losing face of his sister's hoarded coin. It is the world he died for. He has come home.

It is still a four-day walk back to the new capital, and though it seems both illogical and unfair, our reborn hero's feet still throb and sting with blisters in his worn-out army boots. He is warm enough in his old jeans and the blue velvet coat, despite the clouds that roll in from the east, but he walks with a deep internal chill that only deepens the closer he gets to home. He should have kept his ruined shirt to remind him that there is no such thing as a bloodless victory, a bloodless war. The invaders had penetrated too deeply to be shed with the nation's old skin. Like embedded ticks engorged with suddenly poisoned blood, they—men and women of the East and the West, their weapons and machines—have suffered transformation along with the rest of them, and though harmed, they have not been rendered harmless. There are monsters in this new world. He sees one slain, a tank-dragon with bitter-green scales, a six-legged lizard with three heads and one mad Russian face, in the fields near where he had met the checkpoint guards and Martiana Vronskaya on his way north just a few days ago. Perhaps some of these confused and scrabbling warriors are those same young volunteers with their flak jackets and jeans. The jeans have not changed, nor the fearful determination, but the short spears with the shining blades are new. New, and as old as the world. Our hero leaves them to their bloody triumph on the flower-starred field, and like the veteran he is, continues on his painful way.

The new capital has changed more than the old, its modern buildings wrenched into something too much stranger than their origins. Our hero suspects this will never be an easy place to live, not even the old quarter where his sister lives. Here, 18th-century houses have melted like candlewax, or spiraled up into towers like narwhal tusks and antelope horns, crumbling moldings and baroque tiles bent and twisted out of true. Our hero cannot tell if this new architecture is better or worse than the old, uglier or more beautiful. He is only frustrated that the landmarks have changed, and that he cannot figure out where the house is that once he could find blind drunk and staggering. It seems bitterly unfair. He circles the half-familiar streets, until finally a doorway catches his eye, a pale door like a tooth or a pearl, with above it a wholly prosaic glass-and-iron transom in the shape of a fan. He knows that transom, and now that he is looking, he recognizes a brass-capped iron railing, a graffitoed slogan barely legible among the creeping blue flowers on the pavement at his feet. Tears of gratitude sparking hot and wet in his eyes, he turns the corner and walks to the second door.

His key still works, despite the rubies bursting like mush-rooms from the crazed paint on the door. He enters the old-house quiet, breathes in the intimately remembered smell of dry wood and cabbage and sandalwood incense, climbs the crooked, creaking, fern-and-trumpet-vine stairs. He knocks on his sister's door, and she opens it, and she is just the same.

ABOUT THE EDITORS

Founding editor of *Fantasy Magazine*, Sean Wallace has worked full-time for Wildside Press for both its book and magazine divisions since 2001. In between editing the World Fantasy award-winning Prime Books imprint, issues of *Fantasy Magazine*, and volumes of the *Best New Fantasy* and *Horror: The Best of the Year* anthology series, he occasionally plays a mean game of racquetball. He currently lives in Maryland, with his wife, Jennifer, and their two cats, Amber and Jade.

Co-editor of *Fantasy Magazine*, Paul G. Tremblay has also sold over fifty short stories to markets including *Razor Magazine, Chizine, Weird Tales, Interzone, Clarkesworld, Last Pentacle of the Sun: Writings in Support of the West Memphis Three*, and *Horror: The Best of the Year, 2007 Edition*. He is the author of the short fiction collection *Compositions for the Young and Old*, which features an introduction from Stewart O'Nan, and the novella *City Pier: Above and Below*. He has really long, double-jointed fingers and toes, which makes up for his lack of uvula. Other fascinating tidbits can be found at www.paulgtremblay.com.